The *Crazy* Christmas Job Swap

Gary Smith

ISBN-13: 9781701362260

ALSO AVAILABLE

The Supervillain Next Door

Visit <u>www.garysmithbooks.com</u> for more
information!

1

THE NIGHT BEFORE CHRISTMAS

The town of Bridgeton lay still and sleeping beneath a blanket of stars. Streetlights lit up empty pavements with their pale glow, while the only cars on the street were parked and still, their engines cold. Every home was in darkness, the occupants tucked up warm and cosy in their comfy beds.

Stars twinkled in the inky sky and the moon shone brightly. It was a beautiful sight, but the only ones to see it were the snowmen standing still and silent in gardens and parks throughout the town.

Then, something *very unusual* happened.

One of the twinkling stars began to **move!**

It picked up speed as it darted across the sky, pulsing with a sparkling light. Up, down, left, right – the star kept on looping and turning at dizzying speeds.

It eventually came to a halt, as if unsure of its next move. Then it set off in a new direction, its course now confident and sure.

As the star increased in size its light grew ever brighter. Then, carried on the wind, came the sound of tinkling bells and a deep booming laugh.

"HO HO HO!"

Santa Claus had come to town!

A magnificent golden sleigh exploded into view as it soared through the air, pulled by nine gigantic reindeer. The largest, at the front of the sleigh, had a shiny red nose that glowed brightly, lighting up the dark.

"Onwards, Rudolph!" shouted Santa. "We've got lots of houses to visit and not much time."

The reindeer grunted in protest but put on an extra burst of speed. Santa was thrown back in his seat, the large bag of presents behind him wobbling precariously.

"That's it my boys!" he whooped, hauling himself back into his seat and taking a tight grip of the reins. "That's the spirit!"

When the first house came into view Santa tugged on the reins and the reindeer instantly changed direction, hurtling downward and making the sleigh bells jangle furiously. 36 hooves clippety-clopped across the roof before the sleigh touched down with a soft **thump**, scattering snow in all directions as it slowed to a halt.

The reindeer stood and panted, long tongues hanging out as they greedily sucked in great mouthfuls of air. Steamy clouds of warm breath floated upwards, clearly visible in the cold night.

Santa heaved the bag of presents over his shoulder and gave Rudolph an affectionate pat. "You all get some rest. I'll be back in a minute – maybe with a nice juicy carrot."

He tapped his nose twice and then was gone, vanished into thin air. The reindeer didn't even notice; they were too busy arguing about whose turn it was to eat the carrot. Pulling a magical sleigh all over the world was *very* hungry work.

Santa appeared inside the bedroom and stood still for a moment, letting his eyes adjust to the darkness. He pulled a list out of his pocket and ran his finger down it, searching for a particular name.

"Let's see now. Oh yes, Steve Grant. Why you have had a busy year! Your spot on the nice list is well deserved."

Humming a little tune to himself, Santa placed the sack of presents on the floor and reached inside, rummaging around for the correct gift.

He pulled it out with a flourish and examined it with evident satisfaction, running his finger over the perfectly wrapped box. The paper was thick and shiny, topped with a splendid golden bow. "A model boat to go with your glider. Perhaps that neighbour of yours can help you build it?"

He positioned the box so it would be the first thing that Steve saw when he woke up. Then he gleefully clapped his hands together as he spotted the food and drink sitting on the bedside table.

"Oh ho! What do we have here?"

He greedily popped the cookie into his mouth and washed it down with the milk, before using a large red handkerchief to wipe the crumbs from his bushy white beard.

"Delicious! Have a very merry Christmas!"

He picked up the carrot and tapped his nose twice, before vanishing into thin air.

Santa appeared back on the rooftop, and the reindeer licked their lips in anticipation when they spotted their favourite food.

"Here you go, boy," he said, holding out the carrot to Dasher. The huge reindeer snatched it off him eagerly, swallowing it whole before his hungry friends could steal it.

Santa swung his bag of presents into the back of the sleigh and jumped into the driver's seat. Pulling his fur-trimmed hat securely down on his head, he grabbed the reins and held them tight.

"Time to go, boys! There's not much time 'til morning!"

Rudolph and the other reindeer began to move

5

forward, first walking, then cantering, then racing. First the reindeer and then the sleigh lifted into the air, soaring high into the December sky.

The sleigh grew smaller and smaller until all that was left was a bright light darting through the sky, and a faint message carried on the wind.

"Ho Ho Ho. Merry Christmas!"

***

Halfway across the country, in a small house on the outskirts of Manchester, Anna Macleod had finally drifted off to sleep. A tiny white tooth was tucked safely under her pillow.

Hours later, when Anna's parents had gone to bed and the house was all in darkness, a sparkling ball of light appeared in the sky and headed straight for her bedroom window.

The light hurtled towards the window at speed, as if it were planning to break through. Then, at the last second, it stopped before the glass and was still. It tapped against the glass once, twice, three times! Then it pressed against the glass and passed *straight through it* and into the room.

The ball of light spun around in a joyous dance, illuminating toys and posters on its journey before finally coming to a rest above Anna's sleeping form.

The glow faded, but this time there was no reveal of giant reindeer or a golden sleigh. Instead there was a beautiful, impossibly tiny woman, wearing a pink dress and a golden tiara. Her long blonde hair framed a kind face and she smiled as she looked down at Anna, whose slender fingers cradled her jaw as she slept.

An elegant bag with a tooth-shaped clasp hung over her shoulder, while in her right hand she held a long silver wand that was topped with a pink and golden star. But the most unusual thing about this woman was that she was floating in the air, kept aloft by two tiny wings that sprouted from her back.

The Tooth Fairy had come to visit!

"You poor little soul," whispered Adora (for even Tooth Fairies have names). "Does that hurt?"

Adora's wings fluttered faster and carried her towards the pillow that was so much bigger than she. With a wave of her wand the edge of the pillow lifted and the tiny tooth floated out, its white covering smeared with streaks of blood.

Adora smiled as she examined the tooth, as she had done with so many others over the years.

"It's beautiful," she told Anna's sleeping form. "I can tell you've taken such good care of it. I promise that I'll do the same."

With another wave of her wand the bag slung over her shoulder opened and a beautifully shiny £1 coin rose out. It floated over to the pillow and slid underneath, while Adora placed the tooth in the bag.

"Goodbye," whispered Adora. "And thank you for the lovely tooth."

She spun her wand through the air and the sparkling light appeared once more, surrounding her with its vivid glow. The ball of light passed through the window and up into the night sky, eventually fading from sight.

Inside the darkened bedroom, a little girl dreamt of fairies and princesses, her worries now forgotten.

***

Across sea and land, from the largest city to the

smallest village, Santa and the Tooth Fairy worked through the night on this Christmas Eve.

For countless years they had carried out their duties, through rain and snow and through good times and bad. It didn't matter what a child looked like, where they lived or how popular they were. No matter what else was going on in their lives, children all around the world knew that they could rely on Santa Claus and the Tooth Fairy.

Until now, that is. For this was the year that **everything** changed.

And it all began at a party...

2

PARTY AT THE TOP OF THE WORLD

The sky above the North Pole was alive with the brightest colours. Shades of red, green, yellow and purple danced and merged together, creating an unforgettable lightshow.

On the snowy ground below, a lumbering polar bear cast a curious glance upwards before quickly losing interest, returning to the more important business of finding something to eat.

Brainy people would explain that the light show was called the Northern Lights and was caused by charged particles colliding in the upper atmosphere. They would talk about electrons, protons and solar winds, possibly while drawing complicated diagrams.

But remember this important life lesson. Sometimes, brainy people can be *really dumb*.

As every resident of the North Pole knew, the light show taking place that night - and at the same time every year – was **Santa's Christmas party**.

There aren't a lot of parties held at the North Pole. Polar bears aren't very sociable and artic foxes don't like sharing their food. But even if there were a hundred million parties, Santa's would still have been the greatest and most *splendiferous* one of all.

Unlike most Christmas parties, it didn't take place before Christmas. That was Santa's busiest time, when he and the elves were frantically preparing for Christmas Eve.

But when Boxing Day came and the presents had been delivered for another year, that was when Santa and the elves could celebrate in style!

Santa's grotto and workshop were as busy as ever, but with a different kind of activity. Instead of crafting toys and wrapping presents, elves rushed around hanging decorations, placing lights and singing happily.

Santa stood in the middle of the room and watched the preparations take shape, holding a huge mug of hot chocolate and shouting out instructions.

"Luke, these lights need to be higher on the right hand side…. Nedzil, you've hung that decoration upside down… Bromly, why is there smoke coming from the kitchen?"

The elves scurried about, anxious to please. After all, the sooner their jobs were done the sooner they could enjoy the party. And what a party it would be! Anyone who was anyone would be there.

The Tooth Fairy, The Easter Bunny, Sandman, The Man in the Moon, Jack Frost, Father Time, April Fool — all the magical beings that worked so hard to bring joy to children would take one night off to party and have fun together.

And not just them! All their helpers and assistants were invited as well, from apprentice tooth polishers to senior egg painters.

There was enough food to feed several armies, prepared by the finest elf chefs. There were drinks of all types and colours, including Santa's famous hot chocolate recipe. There was karaoke, music and games.

It was the party TO END ALL PARTIES!

You could even say it was *magical*.

***

By 9pm the party was in full swing. It was fortunate that Santa had no neighbours, because the noise levels were through the roof.

A group of elves whooped and cheered as the Easter Bunny showed off his moves on the dance floor, hopping and jumping about the room like he had giant springs on his feet. Tiny fairy imps giggled with delight as they buzzed through the air, enjoying the spectacle.

Santa was stood behind the drinks table, handing out hot chocolate to everyone that passed by. And the Tooth Fairy led an energetic conga line that snaked around the room, growing larger all the time.

From a corner of the room, Luke, Ben and Martin stood and watched the fun. The three of them stood out in the crowded room simply because they looked so *normal*. In a room filled with elves, fairies and giant rabbits, they were three human boys.

Luke was nine years old and tall for his age, already towering over the elves. He had been with Santa since he was five years old, when his Christmas wish had been for a home and a family. Being taken to live at the North Pole wasn't *quite* what he'd expected, but he'd grown to love living with Santa and the elves.

At seven years old, Ben was a little younger but was brave and full of bright ideas. He had short blonde hair, a cheeky smile and golden skin.

(Why was his skin golden? Well, let's just say that if the Tooth Fairy ever tells you to stand back from the tooth polishing machine, make sure you listen to her.)

Martin lived with the Easter Bunny. A quiet boy who was a keen artist, he helped design and decorate the eggs. Surprisingly, despite spending his days surrounded by delicious chocolate, he was still as

14

skinny as a rake. He'd eaten so much chocolate when he first arrived that he had felt sick for days afterwards. As a result, he now stuck to fruit and vegetables.

The boys sipped their drinks as they watched the party continue around them. At times like this they still found it hard to believe that they lived among such magical beings.

Luke pointed towards Santa, who had handed out all his drinks and made his way to the dance floor. His big belly bounced up and down as he danced about, jiggling like a huge bowl of strawberry jelly.

"I'm worried about him," Luke confided in his friends. "I think he's been a little lonely since Mrs Claus left."

"Mrs Claus left?" replied Martin in surprise. "What happened?"

Luke shrugged. "She said that she was tired of it always being so cold here. She's booked herself on a cruise ship for two months."

"If she'd just waited until after Christmas, Santa could have gone with her," suggested Ben.

Luke chuckled. "Oh, there was no chance of that. He doesn't cope well with the heat. Besides, he never takes off his red suit or boots, which would make it hard to get a suntan."

The boys snorted with laughter as they imagined Santa lying on a beautiful sandy beach, drinking hot chocolate while dressed in his thick woollen outfit.

"The Easter Bunny can't take a break either," sighed Martin. "After Christmas is when we start to get really busy, making sure things are all set for the spring."

"And I don't remember the Tooth Fairy ever having a holiday," said Ben. "Boys and girls lose teeth every day, so it's hard to take time off."

"They all work so hard," agreed Luke. "At least they get to have fun tonight. They certainly deserve it."

***

When midnight came around the party was still going strong, but the numbers were much reduced. Tired from dancing, full up with food or with sides aching from laughter, many of the guests had gone to bed or set off on their journey home. Others had simply fallen asleep where they were. Elves lay face down at tables snoring gently, while an exhausted fairy imp had made itself a makeshift bed in a bowl of peanuts.

"Do you think it'll finish soon?" asked Martin as he unleashed a jaw-cracking yawn. "I don't know how much longer I can stay awake."

"Then I've got some bad news for you," replied Luke. "Santa's just wheeled out the Karaoke machine!"

The three boys groaned in unison, knowing what was in store. The Karaoke machine was a regular feature at Santa's parties. With hot chocolate grasped in one hand and microphone in the other, he would belt out song after song.

"C'mon, Santa!" complained the Easter Bunny, his long ears drooping with tiredness. "I think it's a bit late for a singsong."

"Nonsense!" chuckled Santa as he busied himself with checking cords and switches. Then, once satisfied that all was ready, he tapped the microphone and began to speak.

"My friends! Thank you for coming to our annual get together. We've had the most amazing night, and what better way to end than with a singsong! I'll start."

"Gee, what a surprise," the Tooth Fairy whispered to the Easter Bunny.

"This is a song about a very special person – ME! Ho Ho Ho."

With great enthusiasm, Santa began to sing, his booming voice echoing round the room.

"Oh, you better watch out, you better not cry
You better not pout I'm telling you why!
Santa Claus (that's me!) is coming to town.

I'm making a list and checking it twice
I'm going to find out who's naughty or nice
I'm coming to town."

Enjoying himself immensely, Santa skipped around the room, trying to encourage his audience to join in. Although a few elves dutifully clapped their hands, most people just stared at him blankly with tired bloodshot eyes. It had been a *very* long night.

The problem was that although everyone there liked Santa greatly, even his closest friends had to admit that at times he could be *incredibly* big-headed. Because when Santa sang Karaoke, he didn't just hog the microphone. He sang song after song – all of which were about him.

From *Jingle Bells* to *Rudolph the Red Nosed Reindeer;* there was nothing Santa enjoyed more than singing about how much people loved him and how hard he worked.

For the people who had been coming to his parties for years, this was a little tiresome. It's always nice to hear that a friend's doing well, but no one likes a show-off who's too big for their boots.

Santa ended with a big finish; twirling round, leaping into the air then breaking out the jazz hands.

The rapturous applause he was expecting never materialised. The remaining guests were all talking amongst themselves, completely oblivious to his spirited performance.

"AHEM!" interrupted Santa. "How was the song?"

The Easter Bunny looked around somewhat guiltily. "It was really good, Santa. Probably your best one yet."

Santa puffed up with pride. "It was, wasn't it? I'm so lucky to have such wonderful songs written about me. It's nice that people appreciate hard work and effort."

The Tooth Fairy rolled her eyes in exasperation. "Here he goes again! We all work hard – do you think he even knows what he sounds like?"

"Take it from me, Adora," replied the Easter Bunny. "He's been like this for hundreds of years - he's not going to change now."

Oblivious to his friends' lack of interest, Santa continued to hog the microphone. "Does no-one else want to sing? Well, in that case I'll sing another one! Do we have any requests?"

"When Santa got stuck up the chimney!" shouted Adora, a mischievous glint in her eye.

There was a collective intake of breath from the gobsmacked crowd. They all knew better than to mention that song. The elves seated next to the Tooth

Fairy hurriedly moved their chairs away.

"I WAS NOT STUCK!" roared Santa. "I was simply having a little nap in a quiet chimney."

"Of course you were," Adora assured him, trying not to giggle. "Who would possibly think otherwise?"

"ACHOO, ACHOO, ACHOO!"

The Easter Bunny gave Adora a knowing wink as he blew his nose on an oversized white handkerchief. "Excuse me, something must have been tickling my nose."

Santa's eyebrows shot up, and he gripped his microphone tightly as a hushed silence descended upon the room. One particularly nervous elf fainted, landing face down in his bowl of jelly and ice cream. His friends immediately began to argue about who would take him outside for some fresh air. No one wanted to stay to see what happened next.

"You know I don't sing that song," said Santa in a low voice, staring daggers at his two friends.

"Aw, but it's so catchy," chuckled the Easter Bunny. He grabbed Adora's hand and pulled her to her feet, spinning her round the room.

"There's soot in my sack, my nose is all black," he crooned. "Come on, Santa," he called. "You know the words."

Santa didn't join in. He just stood and watched them, growing visibly more annoyed by the second. When the Easter Bunny and Adora noticed his furious expression they stopped mid dance, feeling rather embarrassed with their behaviour. Suddenly, Santa wasn't looking very jolly.

"We're sorry, Santa," Adora apologised, flying over

and putting an affectionate arm around him. "We were just messing around."

"Oh, I know exactly what you were doing," fumed Santa. "You're jealous that people write songs about me. Remind me - how many songs are there about the Tooth Fairy?"

Adora looked crestfallen, and there was an awkward silence that seemed to drag on forever, with none of the guests quite sure what to say.

It was at this point that Luke, Ben and Martin came through from the kitchen. Chatting away happily, their conversation died away as they took in the strange scene between Santa and Adora.

"What's going o-"

Before Ben could finish his question, Adora stormed towards him and grabbed his hand, pulling him after her.

"Come on, Ben. We're leaving!"

"We are?" asked Ben, wondering what was happening.

"YES, WE ARE!"

Ben barely had time to wave goodbye to his friends before Adora marched him out of the room.

"I think it's time we left as well," announced the Easter Bunny, hopping towards Martin. "Thanks for the party, Santa." Then they were gone as well, leaving Luke alone.

He looked at the scene in front of him – the nervous elves and an oddly quiet Santa. "Does this mean that the party's over?" he asked.

Santa punched a number into the Karaoke machine and picked up the microphone once more. "Not at all, my boy. It's just getting started!"

As the familiar tune of *Jingle Bells* began to play, Luke gave a resigned sigh and headed for bed.

3

OLD FRIENDS: NEW FOES

Luke gingerly picked his way through Santa's grotto, carefully stepping over plastic cups, discarded sweet wrappers and snoring elves. The grotto was like a scene from a disaster movie, with clutter and debris littering every inch. But as disgustingly messy as the room was, the clean-up would have to wait. Luke was focused on trying to find Santa.

He had already checked Santa's bedroom, the kitchen, the workshop and the lounge. There had been plenty of mess and some very sleepy elves, but no Santa. He was running out of ideas and was starting to worry. Santa had been in a rotten mood after the Tooth Fairy left, and Luke wanted to make sure he was okay.

Luke prodded a sleeping elf with the toe of his boot. The elf grunted and rolled over, barely managing to crack open his weary eyes.

"Whaddayou want?" he yawned, before his eyes flickered shut again.

"Don't fall asleep!" Luke bellowed, continuing to prod the elf. "I need to know where Santa is!"

The elf slowly raised a tired arm and gestured towards the other side of the room. Then his arm flopped down, followed shortly after by the sound of loud snoring.

Luke let him sleep. He knew exactly where Santa would be.

When Luke entered the stables, the first thing that hit him was the smell. The horrible, throat curdling, nose-pinching, eye-watering smell. Reindeer may look cute, but nine of them together in an enclosed space make some *incredibly* toxic fumes.

Trying to block out the pungent aroma of reindeer

pumps, Luke wandered through the stalls. Most of the reindeer were still sleeping, although a couple had already stirred and were lazily munching on their feed.

Luke found Santa in the last stall, his head resting on Rudolph's rear-end. Luke hoped Santa was just sleeping, and that Rudolph's deadly bottom burps hadn't knocked him out.

"Santa," he called. "SANTA!"

Santa rolled over and raised a hand to shield his eyes from the morning light. His boots were caked in mud and his red outfit was covered in stains and pieces of straw.

"Is the party finished?" he croaked.

"Long finished," Luke told him as he helped him up. "Come on, let's get you cleaned up."

***

One hour later, Santa had changed into fresh clothes and was looking more like his old self again. He sipped on a mug of hot chocolate as Luke updated him on the latest news.

"Things were left in a bit of a mess last night, but it's all in hand. I've given the elves a list of jobs to do, so things should be back to normal soon."

"Good, good," replied Santa, as he gave an enormous yawn and stretched his arms high above his head. "Is that everything?"

Luke handed Santa the morning post and shuffled his feet uneasily. "Actually, there is one thing that I wanted to mention to you..."

"Absolutely. Ask away!"

"It's about the Tooth Fairy. I know that you didn't mean to, but I think she was quite upset when she left the party."

"Upset? What nonsense!" Santa spread his arms wide, expressing his innocence. "I've known Adora for YEARS! Believe me, I would know if she was upset."

Luke recalled Adora's hurt expression as she left the party, and wondered how much Santa remembered of the night. Still, he bit his tongue and kept his thoughts to himself, hoping that Santa knew what he was talking about.

"Ah, what did I tell you," chuckled Santa as he opened a letter and noted the address. "Why, here's a letter from her now!"

His cheerful expression gradually darkened as he digested the letter's contents, his rosy red cheeks turning an angry shade of purple.

"Lazy!" he spluttered.

"Big-headed!" he choked

"A show-off!" he exclaimed in disbelief.

Santa crumpled up the letter and threw it across the room. Then he jumped to his feet and marched towards the door.

"Where are you going?" Luke called after him. "What's the matter?"

"I'm going to thank my 'old friend' for her letter!" Santa shouted as he stomped down the corridor, scattering elves like bowling pins.

Luke ran after him, trying to keep up. He didn't know what had just happened, but it looked like his day wasn't going to get any easier.

***

Ben strolled through the brightly lit corridors of the Tooth Fairy's castle, thinking how lucky he was to be part of such an important job. There had been a few mishaps along the way – turning his skin golden hadn't been the *ideal* start, and the fairy imps were so small that he kept sitting on them. Still, he couldn't think of anywhere else that he'd rather be.

The castle was so magical.

So perfect.

So... *noisy?!*

Ben watched in astonishment as a group of fairy imps hurtled around the corner, their wings fluttering madly. They had their hands pressed tightly over their pointed ears and were shouting at the top of their voices.

"MAKE IT STOP!"

"THAT'S THE WORST THING I'VE EVER HEARD!"

"IS SHE FINISHED? PLEASE LET HER BE FINISHED!"

Before Ben could react, the fairy imps had

whooshed past him and along the corridor. Ben watched them go, wondering what on earth was the matter. They had obviously heard something that they didn't like. Perhaps Zambi had been telling scary stories about tooth decay again. That always gave the imps nightmares.

Ben set off in the direction the imps had come from. The corridor was empty, but he could hear a faint noise coming from the room at the end. It almost sounded like singing.

He cautiously crept forward, swaying and teetering on his tiptoes. When he reached the door the singing had stopped, but he could still hear movement from inside. Gathering his courage, he pushed the door open and found the most unusual sight.

The Tooth Fairy was perched on the end of her bed, holding a battered old acoustic guitar. Her room was normally super tidy, but today every inch of the carpet was completely covered with crumpled bits of paper.

She bit her lip in concentration and strummed a note. The jarring chord was so out of tune that it set

Ben's teeth on edge and made the hairs on the back of his neck stand up.

With a moan of frustration, Adora ripped the top piece of paper from her notebook, crumpled it up and threw it on to the floor. Then she grabbed a new sheet and started scribbling furiously, muttering to herself.

Ben stood in the doorway, transfixed by the strange sight before him. He'd *never* seen the Tooth Fairy act like this before.

He cleared his throat and Adora's head snapped up, her concentration broken. She flashed him a big smile and Ben smiled back nervously.

"Ben, you're just in time," she beamed. "I've done it!"

"Done what?" asked Ben, totally confused.

"Written a song, of course! Santa thinks that he's so great just because people sing songs about him. Well, soon they'll be singing about me instead!"

Ben breathed a sigh of relief as he cleared paper from the chair and sat down. All she was doing was writing a song – how bad could it be?

Then he remembered the terrified imps covering

their ears and suddenly got a *very* bad feeling about what was going to happen next.

Adora strummed a chord and cleared her throat. "I call this one, *The visit of the Tooth Fairy*," she announced.

"Have you ever heard, or have you ever seen
Who's coming to your house at night?
You won't hear a thing, you won't see a thing
Because she's staying right out of sight.

But she'll come into your room, right up to your bed
And she'll float there by your head
Because she wants what's in your mouth.
Your teeth.

Oh she loves them (Your teeth, your teeth)
Oh she needs them (Your teeth, your teeth)
They're the thing she loves the most.

Oh she loves them (Your teeth, your teeth)
Oh she needs them (Your teeth, your teeth)
She even likes them better than beans on toast.
Your teeth."

"Well?" Adora asked, looking at him expectantly. "What do you think?"

There was a *very* awkward silence. Ben tried to pretend he thought she was talking to someone else, before remembering that they were the only two people in the room.

"Honestly?" he replied, not daring to look Adora in the eye. "It makes you sound a little creepy."

Adora let out a squeak and turned a funny shade of pink.

"*I* know you're not creepy!" Ben rushed to reassure her. "But it kind of makes it sound like you sneak into houses to steal teeth."

Ben knew that he should probably stop talking, but his lips seemed to have taken on a life of their own. "The part about beans on toast is a bit weird. It almost makes it sound like you eat teeth!"

Adora was now bright red, one eye beginning to twitch.

"Wait. DO you eat teeth? Then I guess that part can stay, but it still sounds a little creepy. Oh, I know! Maybe you could say that you lick teeth instead?"

"I DO NOT EAT TEETH!!!!!" screamed Adora. "AND I'M NOT CREEPY! I'M THE TOOTH FAIRY – BOYS AND GIRLS LOVE ME!"

"Of course they do!" Ben agreed. "They love you even more than beans on toast!"

Adora burst into tears, flying over to the bed and burying her head in the pillow.

"It's... not... fair!" she sobbed. "I just wanted to have one song about me. You heard Santa boast about having all the good tunes."

"Oh, he didn't mean it like that," Ben assured her. "You know that he thinks the world of you; he just gets a bit carried away sometimes."

Adora sat up and drew her legs up to her chest, holding them tight. "You really think so?" she sniffed, wiping away a tear.

"I know so!" said Ben. "Anyway, don't you worry about that. I've got this morning's post here. Maybe it will help take your mind off things."

Adora took the pile of letters and began opening

them with little enthusiasm. When she opened the second letter a small smile appeared on her lips.

"Why, it's from Santa!" she proclaimed. "Perhaps you're right, he must be writing to apologise."

Ben smiled in relief, hoping that meant things would soon be returning to normal. When he saw Adora's smile replaced by a look of confusion, he had a horrible feeling that he was wrong.

"Boring!" she announced in disbelief.

"Old fashioned!" she squeaked.

"Unpopular!" she shrieked.

Before Ben could ask what the matter was, Adora crumpled up the letter and threw it to the ground. Marching over to the bed, she picked up the guitar and raised it high above her head. Then, in a move that would have been the envy of every rock star, she brought it smashing down on the ground.

KKKKRRRRRAAAAASSSSHHHHHHHHHHH!!!!

Strings popped and wood splintered as Adora brought the guitar down again and again, until it was smashed beyond any hope of repair. Ben watched in disbelief as she threw away the mangled instrument and marched out of the room.

"Where are you going?" he called after her.

"TO GIVE SANTA A PIECE OF MY MIND!" she yelled, before shrinking down, taking to the air and flying out of sight.

4

THE LINE IS DRAWN

It took almost five minutes for a panting and tired Ben to reach the castle's communication room. When he entered, he saw a clearly furious Adora standing in front of the video screen. Her hands were on her hips as she shouted at an equally annoyed looking Santa.

Luke was standing awkwardly behind Santa, looking like he really didn't want to be there. Ben knew just how he felt.

"I am not BORING!" shouted Adora. "Children get money from the Tooth Fairy – that's the way it works! How many toys do you think can fit under a pillow?"

"All I do is drink milk and eat cookies?" roared Santa. "I'd like to see YOU visit millions of homes in one night. I don't even have time for a bathroom break!"

"I don't need a song!" the Tooth Fairy shouted over him. "Because I'm not a **raging egomaniac!**"

"There's nothing wrong with my outfit," Santa protested. "It's cold at the North Pole, and red brings out my eyes."

As Luke and Ben watched the shouting match rage back and forth, one thing became clear. Santa and the Tooth Fairy were so upset, so furious, that they simply weren't listening to anything the other one had to say.

"Well I'm going to show you who's the best at their job," proclaimed Adora.

"Not if I show you first!" countered Santa, sticking his tongue out.

Adora stomped her feet in frustration and pointed an accusing finger at him. "You want the tooth? You can't handle the tooth!"

"Well you've earned yourself a place on the naughty list," announced Santa. "I hope you like coal!"

"GOODBYE!" shouted Adora, turning on her heels

and stalking off.

"GOOD RIDDANCE!" replied Santa, stomping off down the corridor.

Luke and Ben were left alone, staring at each other in slack jawed confusion.

"What the heck just happened?" asked Ben.

"The Tooth Fairy wrote Santa a letter listing all the ways she was better than him," replied Luke. "I really wish she hadn't done that."

"No she didn't," countered Ben, loyally sticking up for his boss. "Santa wrote her a letter saying why HE was better."

"No he didn't," protested Luke. Then, seeing that Ben was about to argue, he held up a placating hand.

"Look, whose fault it is doesn't really matter. The important thing is that we stop them before they do something REALLY crazy. Can you do that?"

"I'll try," replied Ben.

"Then good luck," Luke told him. "I have a feeling that we'll both need it."

Are you curious what was in these letters to make two good friends so upset with each other?

Then read on and find out!

First, let's look at the letter that Santa received:

***

The Old Castle
Fairyland
27th December

Dear Santa:

Thank you so much for inviting me to your party. It was lovely to see all my friends and have fun with them.

Unfortunately, you then spoilt it by being such a big-bellied, big-headed, big-bottomed meanie.

You think you're so great just because you have some songs written about you. Well, I'll let you in on a little secret – **Some of these songs aren't even very good!**

Rudolph the red nosed reindeer is most people's favourite Christmas song, and you're only in that for one line!

You say that you work so hard and deliver millions of presents? Let's be honest – the reindeer do all the work. All you do is drink milk and eat cookies! Looking at the way the buttons are almost popping off your jacket, it's easy to see why you got stuck in that chimney.

You work hard for ONE night and then get to laze

around for the next 364 days! That sounds like a pretty cushy deal. Children's teeth fall out every day, so there are no holidays for me.

What do you even do for the rest of the year? Not wash your clothes, that's for sure. Your red suit smells like reindeer pumps and Brussel sprouts.

Best wishes,

The Tooth Fairy

PS. Next time you have a party, stay away from the Karaoke. You're a **terrible** singer!

***

Crikey. That was a bit rude, wasn't it? Now, let's see what got the Tooth Fairy so upset:

***

Santa's Workshop
The North Pole
27th December

Dear Adora:

Thank you so much for coming to my party. It's always lovely when we get together for a chance to relax and have fun.

I know that you're always terribly busy collecting dirty old teeth, so I was glad that you could make it. Unfortunately, you were such a boring old so and so that you almost killed the party stone dead.

People don't want to be lectured about tooth decay when they're enjoying some yummy treats. And how on earth do you manage to spend so much time talking about teeth? At one point I was so bored that I almost fell asleep standing up!

I'll be honest with you – this sort of thing is EXACTLY why you don't have songs written about you. Boys and girls want someone fun and exciting! It's hard for them to get excited about a dentist with wings.

Even your gifts are boring! A coin under the pillow? **YAWN!** It's just so old-fashioned and unimaginative. Still, I suppose not everyone can be as creative as me. That's one of the many reasons why I'm so beloved.

Best wishes,

Santa

PS. I have never been stuck in a chimney. Anyone who says otherwise is a big fat liar.

5

CHRISTMAS COMES EARLY

For many years, the cycle of work for Santa and his elves had been the same. A steady hum of activity grew busier as December drew near, culminating in a frantic Christmas Eve.

By the time that Christmas Day came around the elves were frizzled and frazzled, exhausted from their efforts to ensure that every boy and girl had the perfect Christmas.

As a reward for their hard work, after the fun and excitement of the Christmas party a grateful Santa normally gave everyone a couple of weeks off.

Time to recharge the batteries.

Time to rest and relax.

Time to get a break from designing toys, wrapping presents, and all the other important duties that the elves had to perform.

At least that's what *normally* happened. This year was a little different...

***

Luke walked towards the great hall; a normal human boy easily identifiable among a teeming crowd of elves. They may have been dressed in similar red, white and green outfits, but even at nine years old Luke was taller than everyone apart from Santa.

The elves chatted and gossiped as they marched along, speculating about why Santa had called them together. Luke was wondering the same thing.

Santa had been holed up in his workshop ever since the argument with the Tooth Fairy. Although Luke had tried to visit, nothing he could say had tempted him out.

The silence had lasted right up until this morning, when the ageing tannoy system had crackled into life.

"THIS IS SANTA. CAN EVERYONE COME TO THE MEETING HALL AT ONCE. THANK YOU."

As the message faded away, an enterprising elf called Nedzil began taking bets on what Santa's announcement would be. By the time that voting had closed, the most popular suggestions were as follows:

- *A Christmas bonus to reward the elves for their hard work* – 63 votes.
- *New fairy lights for the Christmas tree* – 47 votes.
- *Mrs Claus was coming home with presents for everyone* – 23 votes.

There were many other suggestions, from the brilliant to the ridiculous. Nedzil's own guess was that Santa had invented an improved hot chocolate recipe.

Eventually the last elf filed into the hall and the assembled crowd stood before the stage, unsure what was about to happen.

The connecting door to Santa's workshop banged open and he marched through, striding purposefully towards the stage. The mass of confused elves watched in anticipation, waiting for him to speak.

"I suppose you're wondering why I've called you here today," asked Santa, scratching his unruly white beard and dislodging day-old biscuit crumbs.

His question was met with a murmur of agreement and countless nodding heads.

"I've gathered you here because I have an announcement to make. A very important one."

The elves who had voted for a Christmas bonus started nudging each other, grinning from ear to ear.

"You all work hard and do a wonderful job. But let me ask you a question: why do we only deliver presents on Christmas Eve?" Santa turned to one luckless elf, awaiting his answer.

"Because it's the day before Christmas?" answered Bromly, hopefully.

"BECAUSE IT'S THE DAY BEFORE CHRISTMAS!" repeated Santa. "Then let me ask you another question. Why don't we deliver presents the rest of the year?"

By this point Bromly was nervous and sweating,

looking like he wanted the ground to swallow him up. "Because then they wouldn't be Christmas presents?" he guessed.

"Ah, but they would be!" said Santa. "Because they would be delivered by Father Christmas!"

The elves looked at each other in confusion, trying to decipher the meaning of Santa's words. Luke raised his hand and Santa gestured for him to speak.

"Santa, just so we're clear. Are you saying we should deliver Christmas presents at *different times of the year*?"

"That's exactly right," chuckled Santa. "Well done!"

"Okay... What exactly were you thinking? Maybe start a couple of days earlier?"

Santa tapped his nose and winked.

"Think bigger, my boy. Think bigger!"

"Twice a year!" shouted one elf.

Santa raised his hands, gesturing upwards.

"Four times a year!" shouted another.

Grinning, Santa motioned upwards once more.

"Every month?" shouted another, sounding noticeably more worried.

Santa stood on tiptoes and raised both hands into the air, stretching as high as he could.

The elves looked at each other. They suddenly had a *very* bad feeling about where this was going.

"Not twice a year, not every month, not even every week," declared Santa. "I want us to deliver presents... EVERY SINGLE NIGHT!"

All at once the hall was filled with the greatest hullaballoo. Astounded elves turned to their friends to check they had heard correctly. Others began to panic, performing frantic calculations as they tried to work out how many presents would have to be made and prepared.

THUMP THUMP THUMP

The sound of Santa's heavy boots stomping on the stage gradually returned order to the room. Elves bit their lips and tried to keep a lid on their worry, hoping that Santa was just pulling their leg.

Then Nedzil had a flash of inspiration, confident that

he'd spotted a fatal flaw in Santa's plan.

"We can't deliver presents every night, Santa. How will we know what the boys and girls want? They only write to you at Christmas time."

Nedzil's friends slapped him on the back in appreciation, but Santa quickly burst their bubble when he pulled a thick wad of paper from his pocket.

"Do you know what this is?" he asked. "This is the Christmas list that I received from Charlie Cummings. It goes on for six sides of A4 and in it he asks for 213 separate items. I gave him **five** for Christmas.

"We know *exactly* what the boys and girls want. We give them the things that they've already asked for!"

"Oh... I guess that makes sense," replied a dejected Nedzil, wringing his hands together with worry.

"Now, there's no need to panic. I can see that some of you are a little concerned about the extra work, so I'll reassure you. We're not giving presents to *all* children every night. Why that would just be silly! That would be millions of homes!"

247 elves breathed huge sighs of relief.

"We'll work our way round the houses on a schedule. I think a few hundred thousand homes per night is *much* more sensible."

247 elves realised they were in BIG trouble.

Santa stopped and smiled, as if expecting applause. The only response was some half-hearted claps from around the room before the shocked elves trudged towards the exit.

All thoughts of holiday activities were cancelled. Now it was back to work.

"I don't know what's gotten into him," muttered Bromly as he and Luke followed the subdued crowd. "Presents every night! Where'd he get that daft idea?"

"Beats me," Luke replied, although he had a pretty good idea. He was more concerned with another question – what was Santa going to do next?

6

THE TOOTH HURTS

The elves weren't the only ones having to deal with worrying changes. Inside the Tooth Fairy's castle the fairy imps bustled about as normal, but instead of cheery greetings they exchanged worried looks and anxious words.

The castle was normally a place of joy and song, a smile on every face and laughter in the air as the imps carried out their tasks.

Not today.

The reason was so unexpected that the poor imps didn't know what to make of it. They could hardly believe the evidence of their own tiny eyes.

The problem was this: The Tooth Fairy seemed to have lost her passion for teeth!

She still visited houses and exchanged teeth for money, but something was missing, as if some inner spark was gone.

When she returned from visits she no longer took her time examining the new teeth, poring over their every crack and bump. Instead she would sigh gently as she poured them into the tooth polishing machine, before walking away with her head slumped low.

Often, helpful fairy imps would try to cheer her up by presenting her with special teeth they had found – ones that had been polished to a golden sheen or were perfectly shaped and gleaming white.

Adora would glance at them briefly before saying how pretty they were, but it was obvious that her heart wasn't in it.

The fairy imps didn't know what to do. No one loved teeth more than the Tooth Fairy. No one spent more time collecting them, examining them or praising them.

If a person had ever been born for a job then it was Adora, who got to spend every day doing something that she loved.

So why was she so downcast? What had happened?

The fairy imps worried and fretted, gossiped and speculated. Could it be a broken heart? Was she sick? Did she want to find another job?

No one knew, so the fairy imps came up with a plan. They would choose one person to solve the mystery! One person to solve the riddle, fix the problem and save the day!

But who to choose?

The fairy imps scratched their heads and avoided each other's gaze, none of them wanting to volunteer. They never normally minded their small size, but at times like this they couldn't help but feel tiny and rather helpless. This was a BIG problem that was causing them HUGE worry, and to solve it would be a TALL order.

Ben walked around the corner and stopped in his tracks, surprised to find hundreds of fairy imps gazing at him with unnerving grins on their faces.

"Hi guys," said Ben. "Have I missed something?"

***

After the fairy imps filled him in on the situation, Ben made his way towards the Tooth Fairy's study. He knew that whenever she had work to do or a big problem to solve, that was where she went.

He looked around him and saw that both ends of the corridor were completely blocked by fairy imps, massed together and watching him intently. An imp at the front of the crowd gave him a thumbs up and an encouraging nod.

The message was clear: *You can do this*!

Hoping that their faith in him was justified, Ben knocked on the door and stepped inside.

Adora was sprawled on a chair, her feet up on the desk and her gaze directed at the ceiling. The room was quiet, with the only sound being the soft thump of Adora catching the ball that she repeatedly threw into the air.

Here in the privacy of her room, Ben noticed that

Adora had reverted to her 'normal' height – about that of a six-year-old child. When he had first come to live with the Tooth Fairy that had been one of the most surprising revelations: that unlike the fairy imps, she wasn't always tiny.

Adora shrunk herself down for home visits, but otherwise tended to stay in her larger form. Ben wondered if that was another reason why she had child helpers – to give her someone her own size to talk to.

"Tooth Fairy... Adora... Are you okay?" he asked, not quite sure what to say.

Adora didn't reply and kept throwing the ball into the air, so Ben decided to just keep going.

"The fairy imps are worried about you. They say that you seem a little sad about something."

Still the ball was thrown into the air, travelling up and down hypnotically.

"Is it anything to do with Santa?" Ben asked.

Thump.

The ball hit the ground and rolled under the desk as Adora sat up, brushing stray strands of hair away from her face.

"It's sweet of them to worry," she sighed, "but there's really nothing they can do. I suppose part of me is just wondering if this is all needed."

"What do you mean?" asked Ben, looking around. "Your room?"

A wry smile crossed the Tooth Fairy's lips. "No, all this," she replied, gesturing around her. "Everything we do here collecting teeth. Does it really matter?"

Ben felt his stomach tighten into a knot of worry. He'd never heard Adora talk this way before.

"I don't understand," he admitted. "Of course it matters – boys and girls love you."

"Do they?" asked Adora softly. "I thought so, but what if Santa is right? What if they think I'm just a boring old so-and-so who gives them the occasional coin?"

"You can't think that," Ben blurted out, outraged by what he was hearing. "What you do is really important – losing a tooth can be scary, but you make it something that kids can look forward to!"

Ben thought back to the first time he'd lost a tooth. The shock of it falling out, the nervousness of wondering whether a new one would replace it, and the strange butterflies he'd felt in his stomach when he thought that the Tooth Fairy might visit.

"That's what I'd hoped," Adora admitted. "But Santa's right – they don't sing songs about me or even write me letters. Maybe no one would notice if I stopped."

"No!" Ben protested. "You can't stop!" He hurried over to Adora and knelt beside her, taking her hand.

"Santa's letter knocked your confidence – I understand that! But children need you. Do you want to let them down?"

Adora blushed crimson. "Of course not," she answered. "I want to help them."

"Then do it!" urged Ben. "Don't worry about what Santa says – don't worry about what anyone says! What you do is up to you."

Adora was silent for a moment, considering Ben's words. Then she rose from her seat, a determined expression on her face.

"You're right!" she exclaimed. "I'm not going to stop doing this! I help children! I make them happy! And I'm going to keep on doing that!"

"Yes! Brilliant!" shouted Ben, delighted that his pep talk had worked.

"In fact, I'm going to make them happier than ever. Happier than Santa ever could!"

"Okay..." replied Ben. "I suppose we could stretch to a few extra coins on visits."

"Oh, I'm not talking about more coins," laughed Adora. "I'm going to start giving presents!"

"Presents... right," nodded Ben, trying to keep up. "You mean toothbrushes and toothpaste – that sort of thing?"

Adora looked at him as if he had gone totally loopy. "No, I mean presents. Real presents – the bigger the better!"

She stooped to pick up the ball and began throwing it into the air once more.

"Santa thinks that he's the best, but let's see how he

likes it when he's got some competition."

Adora threw the ball towards Ben, who instinctively caught it.

"The Tooth Fairy's back and she's better than ever! Come on, Ben - let's get to work!"

7

THE NEW ROUTINE

Children around the world were confused.

VERY confused.

When you're a grown up the days pass as if they are on fast forward, one season turning into another like a merry go round spinning faster and faster. Almost as soon as one Christmas has ended, it feels as if the preparations for the next one are beginning.

For children it's a different story. Christmas ends and then the days begin to drag, time itself seeming to slow down. And the more that children want Christmas to come, the longer it seems to take.

Or at least that's what normally happens.

But children around the world woke up on the 2nd of January to something entirely unexpected.

Presents.

Lots and *lots* of presents.

Blinking sleepymen away, children tore off wrapping paper and were stunned to discover presents that had been on their Christmas lists; presents they had resigned themselves to not getting.

The children were delighted, each one believing that for Santa to have come back so soon they must have been VERY high up on the nice list.

Logan Burwell awoke to find the new bike he had asked for, gleaming red and with 6 gears.

Hannah May was thrilled to discover the playdoh kitchen she had longed for. Shrieking with delight, she tore off the packaging and set about producing her culinary creations.

The children weren't sure what was going on, but they knew that it was *amazing!*

***

While some children received unexpected Christmas presents, those who had lost teeth also received a big surprise.

Victoria Wells cradled her tooth under her pillow as she fell asleep, lazily dreaming about what she would spend her pound coin on. Perhaps she'd buy some sweets, or maybe put it towards a comic or a toy.

But when she woke in the morning and felt under her pillow, although the tooth was gone there was no sign of any money.

She whipped up bedcovers and frantically tossed soft toys onto the floor as she hunted for the coin, convinced that it must have rolled away.

Victoria searched down the side of the bed, under the covers and on the floor, but there was no sign. Sitting on her bare bed, shivering in her spotty pyjamas, she decided that the Tooth Fairy mustn't have left any money this time.

She felt a horrible tightness in her chest and a lump in her throat as she tried to fight off tears. Had her tooth not been clean enough for the Tooth Fairy? Had it not been good enough?

But then through the mist of tears she spotted something sitting on her chest of drawers – a small square present wrapped in bright pink wrapping paper.

Victoria stepped out of bed and slipped her bare feet into her slippers, before padding over and picking it up.

Hesitantly, she tugged the edge of the bow and the delicate paper unfurled to reveal a blue jewellery box. Victoria opened it gently and gasped as she saw the beautiful golden bracelet inside.

Half convinced that she was dreaming, she lifted it out to examine and spotted the initials **T.F** etched into the underside of the box.

"Thank you," Victoria whispered. "Thank you so much!"

***

Santa and the Tooth Fairy were both delighted with their new ways of working, feeling *very* pleased with themselves. Unfortunately, not everyone was as happy.

The reindeer were particularly unimpressed. They were having to fly all over the world on a nightly basis without even getting a carrot for their trouble. Not expecting any night-time visitors, children weren't leaving out the traditional Christmas offering.

Santa's elves weren't much happier. They were having to work *incredibly* hard to produce so many toys, hammering, painting and wrapping until they stumbled to bed and fell straight asleep.

"Don't worry," Luke tried to reassure his friends. "I'm sure Santa won't do this for long."

But, in truth, he wasn't sure how long it would go on for. How far *would* Santa go to win his argument with the Tooth Fairy?

In the Tooth Fairy's castle, Ben was wondering the same thing. The Tooth Fairy was delighted with how happy her presents were making children, but the fairy imps were finding the new routine a bit of a struggle.

Lifting a £1 coin is easy, even if you are a tiny fairy imp. Lifting skateboards, bicycles and play kitchens is *much* trickier.

The imps loved the Tooth Fairy and wanted to do all they could to help her, but they all hoped that this would be a very short-lived change.

The exhausted imps were sitting in the canteen, lined up at tables and enjoying their custard. Actually, 'enjoying' isn't quite right. For many of the tired imps slumped at their tables, even lifting their spoon seemed to be too much effort.

Ben watched them closely. Although their weariness was plain to see, the Tooth Fairy didn't seem to notice. She was chatting away ten to the dozen, waving her spoon about as she recounted the story of her most recent visit.

The fairy imps at her table tried to be polite and nod and smile at the right places, but for one poor fellow it was all too much. Succumbing to sleep, he landed face down in his custard. He began snoring gently, sending tiny yellow bubbles floating to the surface.

Ben was tempted to have a nap as well, but then his mobile phone began to ring. He glanced at the caller display and was surprised to see that it was Luke – they hadn't spoken since the angry confrontation between Santa and the Tooth Fairy.

"Hi Luke."

"Hi Ben. I just wanted to phone and say that there are no hard feelings."

"That's okay," replied Ben, pleased to hear from his friend. "I think we both know that Santa and the Tooth Fairy could have behaved better."

There was a pause on the other end of the line. "Hold on," said Luke, sounding confused. "What are you talking about?"

"The argument between Santa and the Tooth Fairy. You said it was Adora's fault, remember?"

"That's not why I phoned. I wanted you to hear it from me before you heard it from anyone else. Santa's delivering presents every night now – we've never worked so hard here."

"HE'S DOING WHAT?" shouted Ben, waking the dozing fairy imp with a start. He raised his custard-splattered face and looked around in bemusement, much to the amusement of his friends.

"I know it sounds crazy, but that's what he's told us to do. I hope the Tooth Fairy won't be too upset."

"Oh, she won't be," replied Ben confidently. "Because we've brought in some changes as well. She doesn't give children money anymore; she gives them presents!"

"Presents?" repeated Luke in astonishment. "The Tooth Fairy doesn't give presents!"

"She does now!" Ben replied.

There was silence for a second before the friends began to laugh, the tension between them broken.

"I can't believe it," chuckled Luke. "Santa was so pleased with himself. I don't think he'll like hearing this."

"The Tooth Fairy won't like it either. How are we going to stop them acting like such big kids?"

"I think we just have to let them get on with it," mused Luke. "Hopefully they'll soon realise how silly they're being."

The two friends said their goodbyes, hoping that the

feud would soon blow over and everyone could be friends again. Unfortunately, that comforting thought didn't last more than a couple of hours.

When Santa and the Tooth Fairy heard what the other was doing, it only made them more determined to carry on. Santa vowed to work even harder, visiting thousands of homes every night, while Adora declared that her presents would become bigger and better.

With reindeer, fairy imps and elves on the brink of exhaustion, and with Santa and the Tooth Fairy still feuding, Luke and Ben feared it would only be a matter of time before something went wrong.

That's *exactly* what happened. And when things went wrong, they went REALLY wrong.

8

NEVER WORK WITH CHILDREN OR ANIMALS

Luke rubbed his numb hands together, trying to coax some heat into his frozen fingers. It was a cold night and he and Santa had been delivering presents for hours without any breaks.

Spurred on by news of the Tooth Fairy's new routine, Santa had declared that he would deliver presents to even *more* houses. To help speed things up he was now taking helpers out with him, to assist with sorting presents and keeping the reindeer happy.

Tonight was Luke's turn. He'd been excited at first,

delighted to finally have the chance to ride in Santa's fabled sleigh. But Santa was so focused on delivering presents that he barely noticed Luke was there, while the reindeer were tired and bad tempered.

By the time they had flown halfway around the world and delivered thousands of presents, Luke was tired, bored and *very* cold, ready to head back to the North Pole.

Unfortunately, Santa had other ideas.

"Right, 47 Janvier Street," he muttered to himself as he steered the sleigh downwards towards the house. "Little Tony Atkinson."

The heavy sleigh bumped down onto the flat roof and slid through the thawing ice, spraying slush in all directions. Before it had fully stopped, Santa jumped into the back seat and began to rummage in the sack of presents.

Luke watched him curiously. "What are you doing, Santa? Don't you normally take the sack in with you?"

Santa turned around in surprise, as if noticing Luke's presence for the first time.

"Yes, but Tony's present is a little different from the rest," he explained.

Santa lifted something out of the sack and Luke gasped as he realised what it was – a tiny cocker spaniel; fluffy, golden and very cute!

"Has that been in the sack the whole time?" he asked. "How did you do that?"

Santa chuckled, giving Luke a momentary glimpse of the Santa of old, who was always jolly and light-hearted.

"That's a family secret, my boy. But don't you worry, he's perfectly safe and well. Aren't you, puppy?"

Santa bent over and tickled the puppy behind the ear. It dipped its head to one side and panted happily, enjoying the attention.

"I'll be back in a minute," Santa told Luke. "I'll just get this little one settled in."

When Santa appeared in Tony's bedroom, he looked around for the best place to put the puppy and its bed. Choosing a spot in front of Tony's bookcase, Santa made sure the sleeping puppy was comfortable and prepared to magic himself up to the roof.

But then he heard a noise from the next room and froze as still as a statue, listening intently. His first thought was that the voices belonged to Tony's parents, but then he realised that one voice sounded *very* familiar.

"It can't be..." he muttered to himself as he crept into the hall, following the sound of conversation and forgetting all about the tiny puppy. It woke from its nap and looked around in confusion, wondering where it was. Then, spotting Santa, it clambered over the edge of its bed and began to pad after him.

Arriving at the bedroom door, Santa pushed it open a crack and peered through the gap. He could hardly believe the sight that met his eyes!

The Tooth Fairy and Ben were stood at the side of a little girl's bed, with Ben holding on to the reins of a shimmering pink unicorn. They were talking in loud whispers, trying not to wake the young girl.

"All I'm saying is that maybe a unicorn is a little big," said Ben. "It takes a lot of magic to make something like this, and you need to save some for your other presents."

"We have to go big, Ben!" Adora protested. "Coins are boring, remember?"

"AHA!" shouted Santa as he dived into the room. "Caught you! Thought you'd try and sabotage my present, did you?"

Adora looked at him in astonishment. "What are you doing here?" she asked. "Can't I even collect teeth in peace anymore?"

Seeing Santa's obvious confusion, Ben helpfully gestured towards the bed. Penny, Tony's younger sister, lay face down on her pillow, snoring gently.

"You don't expect me to believe that your ending up in the same house as me is a coincidence?" Santa asked, sounding considerably less certain than before.

Adora gave him an exasperated look and opened her grip to reveal a tiny white tooth, freshly collected from under Penny's pillow.

"Well?" she asked, her hands on her hips.

Santa felt terribly embarrassed and more than a

little guilty, but his pride wouldn't let him be the first to apologise. "We can't both turn up at the same house," he huffed. "We'll have to decide on a schedule."

"A schedule?" scoffed Adora. "I can't *decide* when children's teeth fall out. It's you who's delivering presents when you shouldn't be!"

"Don't talk to me about presents!" Santa snapped back. "Is that a real-life unicorn? Where do you think she's going to keep that? In her toy cupboard? Maybe take it into her school for show and tell?"

"I can't win!" shouted Adora. "First my presents are too boring, then they're too big! You're IMPOSSIBLE!"

"And you're INFURIATING!"

Ben tried to keep the unicorn calm as Santa and the Tooth Fairy continued to argue. It was growing increasingly agitated, shaking its head in irritation as if trying to shake off a persistent fly. He tightened his grip on the reins and hoped that the two would stop arguing soon.

***

The puppy had enjoyed its journey through the cavernous hall. There were so many wonderful smells that made its nose twitch, and it had done a lovely big wee all over a gigantic bookcase.

Following the sound of voices, it padded into the bedroom and its tail shot up in excitement as it spotted something *very* big, *very* pink and *very* tasty.

Trying to sound as intimidating as possible, the tiny puppy ran towards the unicorn as fast as its little legs could carry it, barking and yipping the whole time.

Such a tiny dog wouldn't have done any harm to the huge unicorn, but the arrival of this new pest nipping at its heels was the last straw.

The startled unicorn whinnied in terror, rearing up and almost knocking Ben to one side. Then it turned on its heels and charged towards the window.

With one mighty leap it smashed through the glass. His hand still caught in the reins, Ben was dragged along behind it. Then something remarkable happened.

Instead of plummeting to the ground the unicorn

soared into the air, leaving a shimmering trail of rainbows and sparkles in its wake.

Santa and Adora looked at each other in horror. Their visits were meant to be quiet and in secret; they were *not* meant to involve smashed windows and runaway unicorns.

"That's why you don't give puppies as Christmas presents!" shouted Adora, hurrying towards the ruined window and scanning the sky for any sign of Ben.

"Oh, and I suppose that flying unicorns are SO much better!" grumbled Santa.

Then, several things happened at once.

From outside they heard a roar, a shout and then the sound of Santa's sleigh sliding along the roof, its bells jangling madly.

In the bed next to them, Penny stretched and yawned, beginning to wake up.

And from further down the corridor they heard the children's father grumbling to himself as he hauled himself out of bed, coming to see what the noise was.

"This is not good!" whispered Adora.

Santa's sleigh zoomed past the window, quickly followed by Ben and the unicorn. Only Luke's legs were visible, sticking out of Santa's sack, while Ben was hanging on to the unicorn's reins for dear life.

"It's really not," agreed Santa.

9

UP ON THE ROOF

The reindeer waited patiently on the icy roof, enjoying the rare opportunity to have a rest. Bored and cold, Luke had moved towards the back seats of the sleigh, debating whether he should do something a little bit naughty.

Luke knew that he shouldn't touch Santa's sack, but he was finding it hard to fight his curiosity. Just how did it manage to hold thousands of presents? Was it like a T.A.R.D.I.S., bigger on the inside?

Deciding that Santa wouldn't mind if he had one quick peek, Luke pulled open the sack and bent over.

As he did so he heard an ear-splitting **CRASH** as the startled unicorn burst through the window and rose into the air, flying upwards in a panic and dragging Ben behind it.

With their majestic horns and flowing manes, unicorns may look cute, but there's one thing that shouldn't be forgotten.

Unicorn horns are sharp.

Sharp and *very* pointy.

By the time the unicorn noticed the sleigh, it was too late to change direction. It collided with the unsuspecting reindeer at full speed, its horn jabbing Comet right in the middle of his hairy bum.

"GAROOOOOOHHHHHHHHH!!!!!!!!!!"

Comet roared in surprise and reared into the air, dragging the other reindeer with him.

The sleigh rocked and bucked as it jerked into the air, throwing Luke forward into Santa's sack of presents.

"Wooaaaaaaaahhhhhhhhhh!"

Luke desperately reached out, managing to grab on to both sides of the sack. He was left hanging face downwards, his feet sticking out of the sack and dangling in the air. His initial relief at saving himself soon turned to amazement, and his stomach churned like a whirlpool as he saw what lay before him.

The sack WAS bigger on the inside. Gifts of every shape and size stretched out before him for what seemed like miles. He swallowed hard as he realised how far he would fall if he lost his grip.

"Santa, I need a hand please," he called, trying not to panic.

An almighty jolt jarred Luke's right hand loose and he reached out in desperation, with his grasping fingers managing to grip the slightest piece of fabric.

As Luke's arms began to ache with the strain, he decided that now was actually the *perfect* time to panic.

"SAAAAAAANNNNNNNNNNNTTAAAAAAAAA!" he called. **"HELLLLLLLPPPPPPPPPP!!!!!"**

***

Ben's night wasn't going any better. With his hand still caught in the reins, he was being dragged all over the sky as the frightened unicorn tried to make its escape.

"Good unicorn!" he shouted, trying to make himself heard over the roar of the rushing wind. "Put me down and I'll give you a nice sugar lump."

The unicorn turned its head, appearing to notice him for the first time, and Ben smiled in relief. Then it dipped its head and lunged towards the dangling reins.

Ben was initially confused, wondering what it was trying to do, but then he noticed the way it angled its horn and it suddenly made sense.

THE UNICORN WAS TRYING TO CUT THE REINS!

"Mr unicorn," he called. "I'd really rather you didn't do that. Not all of us can fly, you know."

Could the unicorn not hear him over the wind, or did it just not listen? All Ben knew was that it kept on rubbing its horn against the reins, the leather fabric becoming more and more frayed until eventually...

The reins SNAPPED!

Ben tumbled downwards, plummeting through the sky as the unicorn soared through the air and out of sight.

10

SLEIGH DRIVING FOR BEGINNERS

Inside the ruined bedroom, Santa and the Tooth Fairy were still arguing about who was to blame for the unfolding disaster.

"This is terrible!" groaned Santa. "Your unicorn has scared my reindeer away."

"MY unicorn?" spluttered Adora. "It was your puppy that scared it away in the first place!"

The argument might have continued to rage back and forwards if Penny hadn't let out a huge yawn that echoed round the room. Santa and Adora instantly froze as they watched Penny turn over and pull her covers up tight.

"Okay," whispered Adora. "Never mind whose fault it is. We have to fix this before anyone finds us here."

"Right," agreed Santa. "Good plan!"

"You help Ben and get your reindeer back, and I'll make sure that things get fixed in here."

"Slight problem with that plan," admitted Santa. "You *do* remember that without my reindeer I can't actually fly?"

Adora sighed in exasperation. "Fine! *I'll* rescue Ben while *you* tidy things in here. Just don't make things worse!"

She shrank down and flew out into the chill night, her tiny wings fluttering in a furious blur.

"As if I would!" Santa shouted after her. "I'm a professional!"

"A professional what?" asked a small voice from beside him.

Santa turned around to see a sleepy Penny sitting up and rubbing her eyes. He slapped his forehead in frustration, hoping that Adora was safely out of sight.

The puppy padded over and rubbed itself against Santa's heavy boots, as if trying to cheer him up.

"Is that a puppy?" squealed Penny. "I can't believe you've brought me a puppy! Is the Tooth Fairy sick? Is that why you're here?"

"Not exactly. You see, I'm actu- "

"THAT'S NOT FAIR!"

Tony stood in the doorway with his arms folded tightly across his chest, looking tremendously unhappy as he watched his sister play with the tiny dog.

"Santa, you didn't give me the dog I wanted for Christmas and now you give one to her! She doesn't even like dogs – she prefers unicorns and horses and all that girly stuff!"

Tony ran past Santa and knelt on the floor, patting his knees as he tried to encourage the puppy to come towards him. The little dog looked from side to side as Penny and Tony both tried to coax it closer, unsure what to do. Unable to decide, it began to chase its tail instead, spinning round and round in circles.

With their new playmate otherwise occupied, the two children turned towards Santa with expectant looks on their faces. He was about to attempt an explanation when he heard a cough from behind him. Turning around he saw Mr Atkinson standing there in slippers and dressing gown, waving a golf club in his direction.

"I don't know who you are," he announced, keeping the golf club pointed at Santa. "But I want you to get out of my house *right now*."

Mr Atkinson pulled his dressing gown cord tighter, as if suddenly realising how cold the room was. Then he looked round and his mouth fell open in amazement as he saw the huge hole in the wall. There was a jagged space where the window used to be; bricks covered the floor, while glass and wood littered the garden below.

"MY HOUSE!" he moaned, rushing over to inspect the damage. "What have you done to my lovely house?"

Santa had years of experience at calming down upset children, so put on his most reassuring voice.

"Oh, don't worry," he told Mr Atkinson. "That'll be easily fixed."

"Easily fixed?" repeated Mr Atkinson in disbelief. "EASILY FIXED?"

Mr Atkinson's face had turned a funny purple colour, with one eye beginning to twitch erratically.

"It won't be easily fixed – there's a flipping great hole in the wall! How did you even *do* that? The whole point of being a burglar is that you break in without anyone noticing. YOU DON'T DESTROY HALF THE HOUSE!"

"*Excuse me!*" interrupted Santa, who by this point was feeling rather offended. "I am *not* a burglar."

"Well what are you then?" asked Mr Atkinson, looking at him suspiciously. "Oh, don't tell me - you're some crazy old man who thinks he's Santa Claus."

"Of course not," Santa reassured him.

"Well, good."

"I *am* Santa Claus."

Mr Atkinson looked Santa up and down, taking in his red outfit with the fur trim, and his trusty black boots. From their vantage point beside the bed both Penny and Tony nodded their agreement.

"You're Santa Claus?" repeated Mr Atkinson, who by this point was seriously considering the idea that he was dreaming. "Prove it."

"Very well," agreed Santa. He thought for a second and then began to talk.

"Your name is Martin Atkinson and you're 41 years old. The first letter you wrote to me was when you were six years old – you asked for a BMX bike. When you were aged eight you were on the naughty list because you played some rather cruel tricks on your teacher. When you were aged 10 you asked for a Micro Machines playset. And the last letter you wrote to me was when you were aged 12, when you asked for a GX4000 console."

Tony and Penny applauded enthusiastically, delighted with Santa's demonstration. Mr Atkinson simply stood there with his mouth hanging open. He no longer thought he was asleep; now he thought he was going absolutely round the twist.

"You're Santa," he stammered. He tentatively reached out and touched Santa's suit, as if expecting it to dissolve at his touch. As he ran his hand down the soft wool his expression of confusion turned to one of astonishment and then delight.

There's something magical that happens when a grown up embraces their inner child. When they can forget about the worry and stress of being an adult and simply feel the joy of the here and now.

"YOU'RE SANTA!" Mr Atkinson cheered, running towards his children and pulling them close. "Look kids, it's Santa!"

"We know, Dad!" replied his embarrassed offspring as they struggled to escape his embrace. "We did tell you that."

"So you did, that's right. A visit from Santa in January! You kids must have been extra good!"

The children beamed with pride and Santa saw his chance. "Oh yes, they've been absolutely wonderful. Top class children! The nice list is full to bursting with all the tremendous things they've done."

Mr Atkinson pulled his children close and wrapped them up in an enormous bear hug, a tear glistening in his eye. "You wonderful kids! You splendid children! Daddy's so proud of you!"

"And so you should be," Santa assured him. "Now, I really am sorry about all the mess. I'll get my best elves to come out and make it as good as new."

Penny, who had been hoping for a spectacular display of magic, looked downcast. "Can't you do it, Santa?" she asked hopefully.

Santa chuckled. "I probably could, but it might get pretty messy." He held up his large hands and wiggled his sausage-like fingers. "The elves do the delicate jobs like wrapping presents and building things, but my hands *are* perfect for handing out presents."

"Well... okay then," said Mr Atkinson, still feeling a little downhearted but trying to remain positive. "I suppose we could live with a hole in the wall for a little while. At least it's not snowing."

"Excellent!" Santa exclaimed. "Now, why don't we get to know each other over some milk and cookies."

***

Adora hurtled through the night sky at top speed, following the shimmering traces of rainbow trail that hung in the air and snaked into the distance.

Far ahead she could make out the unicorn and the silhouette of someone dangling beneath it, swinging wildly from side to side.

"Hang on, Ben," she muttered. "I'm coming for you."

Adora flapped her wings harder, powering herself through the air. The unicorn loomed closer and she was almost within touching distance when an almighty gust of wind slammed into her and sent her tumbling head over heels, leaving her totally disorientated.

When she managed to regain her bearings she saw Santa's sleigh hurtling through the sky, turning and twisting at dizzying speed. Unsure what was happening and not used to being without a driver, the agitated reindeer didn't know what to do.

Adora could make out Santa's bag of presents on the back seat, but there appeared to be something unusual about it. Flying closer to the sleigh she saw what it was – a pair of legs was sticking out of the sack!

Muffled shouts from within the bag told her who the legs belonged to. "Don't worry, Luke. I'm coming!" she yelled.

But before Adora could move, she heard a terrified shout from above and saw Ben falling through the air, turning head over heels as he hurtled towards the ground.

Who to save? Adora had only a split second to decide.

She gripped her wand tighter and flew towards Santa's sleigh as fast as she could go. She drew closer bit by bit, her tiny wings beginning to ache with the strain, until she reached the sleigh and pulled herself on to the driver's seat.

Adora didn't know much about reindeer, but she did know what their favourite food was.

CARROTS!

She raised her wand into the air and waved it from side to side. The air seemed to shimmer and then the image of a gigantic carrot appeared in front of Rudolph. It was a vivid orange colour and looked plump and exceedingly tasty.

Rudolph smacked his lips and veered towards the carrot, pulling the other reindeer with him. Concentrating hard, Adora maintained the illusion so that it was always just out of his reach.

His attention fixed on the elusive carrot, Rudolph chased it all over the sky before hurtling downwards in pursuit. Adora looked up and, after making a quick calculation, moved the image to the left.

Rudolph followed and seconds later there was a shout and then a loud **BUMP** as Ben dropped straight into the seat next to Adora.

"What happened?" he groaned, looking around in confusion. Then he realised where he was and his eyes widened in shock.

"Oh my GOSH! Did you steal Santa's sleigh? He's going to be so mad at you!"

"It's a *very* long story," replied a relieved Adora. "I'm just glad you're okay – as soon as we get back to the castle I'm going to give you some wings of your own."

Ben beamed with pleasure, before a noise from the back of the sleigh caught his attention. "Can you hear something?" he asked.

Adora blushed and jumped up from her seat: "Oh no – Luke!" She flew towards the back of the sleigh, with Ben hurdling over seats to join her. Growing to her full height, she and Ben each grabbed a leg and pulled as hard as they could.

With a loud **POP**, Luke flew out of the bag and landed in a heap on the floor.

"Thank you very much," he gasped as he stared up at his friends. "Take my advice – do NOT look in the sack."

Luke clambered to his feet and looked around at the houses and lampposts that whizzed past them at increasing speed.

"Hold on," he asked. "If we're all back here, who's steering the sleigh?"

Before anyone could reply there was a loud **BANG**, an ear-splitting scraping noise and an impact that made the whole sleigh judder violently, throwing the friends to the ground.

When they clambered to their feet, they saw that the reindeer were wedged inside a small room. The sleigh teetered on the edge of the building, with the back end of it hanging over the destroyed wall.

The shocked faces of Penny, Tony, Mr Atkinson and

Santa looked back at them.

Distraught with the new damage to his house, Mr Atkinson looked about him in disbelief. The window and most of the surrounding wall were missing, and the sleigh runners had cut large grooves in the carpet. Prancer had also contributed to the mess by doing a steaming great poo. The smell didn't put off Penny and Tony, who shrieked with excitement as they ran forward to pet the reindeer.

Santa looked crossly at the Tooth Fairy, before picking up the tiny puppy and giving it to Mr Atkinson to hold.

"I really am *very* sorry about all this mess," he told him. "As I said, I'll get my finest elf craftsmen to come here straight away."

Santa gestured for the other three to move along, before sitting in the driver's seat and picking up the reins.

"Oh, there is one other thing," he announced, turning to Mr Atkinson. "If you could keep what happened tonight to yourselves – we're not really meant to meet people on our visits."

Mr Atkinson nodded. He was hardly listening, unable to stop staring at the devastation that surrounded him.

"Marvellous! Well, bye then. Merry Christmas!"

The reindeer carefully turned around and pulled into the air, leaving the Atkinsons and their ruined home behind.

"Well, that was a fun evening," said Ben, trying to break the awkward silence. "Maybe we should do joint visits more often!"

Neither Santa or the Tooth Fairy replied, causing Luke and Ben to exchange worried glances. Tonight had been one disaster after another – what was going to happen next?

11

HOPPING MAD

"She ruined the whole night!"

Santa restlessly paced around the room, the thump of his heavy boots echoing off the grotto's wooden floors.

The Santa portrayed on Christmas cards and in films always looks the same. His uniform is bright red with snow white trim, his cheeks are as red as rosy apples and he has a happy cheerful face.

The Santa stomping around the room, waving his arms around and ranting to himself, did *not* look like that.

His outfit was messy, covered with the crumbs and stains of countless meals eaten in a hurry. His oversized boots were unpolished and scuffed, while his bushy white beard was scraggy and unkempt.

Santa looked like he *really* needed a holiday.

In comparison, the Easter Bunny was the picture of relaxation. Dressed in his normal outfit of paint-splattered green dungarees, he sprawled on a chair and nibbled on a gigantic carrot as he patiently waited for Santa to calm down.

"I had it all under control! The children were happy and so was their father. Then she somehow managed to crash *my sleigh* into the house! My poor sleigh! And she's meant to be the expert flyer!"

With an exasperated moan, Santa threw his arms up in the air and set off around the room once more.

The Easter Bunny finished his carrot and sprang to his feet. Hopping over to Santa, he placed one furry arm around his old friend's shoulders.

"Santa, you have to try and calm down. Come on, isn't this whole contest getting a little childish?"

"She started it," whined Santa.

"Maybe she did, maybe she didn't. I'm not taking sides, you're both my friends. And you and Adora are friends as well, something that you seem to be forgetting."

"I know that," replied Santa, sulkily jutting out his bottom lip.

"Then why are you even doing this silly contest? Come on, you're both good at what you do. Can't you be happy with that?"

The Easter Bunny smiled at Santa, trying to reassure him. "I know you got your feelings hurt, but think of it this way. None of us came into our jobs for the fame, did we? We did it to make children happy!"

Santa trudged over to his battered old armchair and flopped down in it, looking utterly exhausted.

"I suppose you're right," he admitted. "That's all I've ever wanted – to make Christmas a special time for boys and girls."

"Then keep it special," urged the Easter Bunny, hopping over to join him. "Think about it. If Christmas happens every day then it's not special anymore – it's just normal!"

He laughed and began to juggle four beautifully painted chocolate eggs that he had produced from the seemingly bottomless pockets of his dungarees. "I know that I couldn't deliver eggs every day – it takes time to get them looking this good!"

The Easter Bunny threw the eggs higher and higher, keeping them whirling and twirling through the air. "Let's face it, Adora is the only one of us that can work all year round. After all, she can't decide when children's teeth fall out."

"I know," sighed Santa. "As long as children eat sweets, they'll keep on losing their teeth."

Santa relaxed in his armchair and watched the eggs soar through the air. It was almost hypnotic, and he found his eyes beginning to close. He had been working nonstop for days and he was so very *tired*. Then his eyes snapped open and he sprang out of his chair, pointing an accusing finger at his friend.

"I should have known!" he shouted. "You're on her

side!"

Startled, the Easter Bunny lost his concentration and the eggs fell to the ground, rolling across the floor. Santa bent to pick one up and examined it closely, running his fingers across the detailed painting.

"How do children lose their teeth? They eat too many sweets – too much *chocolate*."

The Easter Bunny retrieved the final egg from underneath the table and bounced to his feet. "You do know that I've no idea what you're talking about."

"I'm talking about your eggs," Santa told him, his eyes narrowing. "Your sugary, delicious eggs."

"Yes, they are rather good," replied the Easter Bunny, beaming with pride. "What about them?"

"I want you to stop delivering them," declared Santa, folding his arms across his chest.

The Easter Bunny burst out laughing, his long whiskers quivering. Then he saw the look on Santa's face and paused. "Wait, you're serious? I can't do that!"

"Of course you can," Santa assured him. "You're friends with both of us, so you shouldn't take sides. And if you deliver eggs then you're helping Adora."

"But delivering eggs is what I do!" declared the shocked rabbit. "That's like asking you to stop delivering toys! Anyway, kids get sweets from lots of different places – even you deliver selection boxes!"

The Easter Bunny was right, of course. Most children will always find a way to seek out yummy treats, no matter how bad they are for their teeth. But Santa was tired and upset, not listening to reason.

"I'm going to ask you one more time you big-eared backstabber – stop delivering eggs!"

"*I will not!*" replied the Easter Bunny, clutching his precious eggs protectively to his chest.

"FINE! Well, you asked for this!" Santa pulled a silver whistle from his pocket and blew three sharp blasts, causing the Easter Bunny to cover his sensitive ears.

Within seconds six elves ran into the room, each one holding various wrapping supplies.

"Get him, boys," instructed Santa. "Design 3B."

The elves advanced on the startled bunny, whose long ears drooped low as he backed away.

"Come on guys, let's talk about this. Let's not do anything hasty!"

Realising that his pleas were falling on deaf ears, the Easter Bunny attempted to leap to safety. His powerful legs helped him jump over the heads of the group, but one quick-thinking elf managed to use his tinsel like a lasso. It wrapped around the Easter Bunny's leg and pulled him down to the ground.

The elves swarmed over him in a flash, using all the skills they had learnt in their many years of wrapping presents. Paper was wrapped over every inch, Sellotape and tags were applied, and tinsel was used to give the perfect finishing touch.

When they had finished the Easter Bunny was almost completely covered, with only his eyes, nose and mouth visible. He tried to flex his arms or jump free, but the tinsel had him wrapped tight and the thick wrapping paper was exceedingly hard to tear.

"Okay Santa," he laughed nervously. "You've had your little joke. You can untie me now."

"Don't worry, it won't be for long. Just until I can win

this competition with Adora."

"I thought we'd agreed that you were going to stop?" moaned the Easter Bunny.

"I'll stop when I win," Santa assured him. "Now if you'll excuse me, I have some presents to deliver."

Leaving his friend wrapped up like an oversized soft toy, Santa headed towards the stables to deliver yet more presents.

12

ONE OF OUR BUNNIES IS MISSING

Martin was worried.

That wasn't unusual. Martin was a rather nervous child who tended to worry about the smallest thing, such as whether he had put the lid back on the toothpaste or had written his thank you letters quickly enough.

But today there was a *big* problem for Martin to worry about.

THE EASTER BUNNY WAS MISSING!

He wasn't in the gallery, wearing a painter's smock and lovingly decorating eggs.

He wasn't in the lush green meadow, basking in the sunshine as he checked that eggs were the perfect shape for rolling.

He wasn't to be found among the noise and smells of the kitchen, tasting chocolate samples and perfecting the most delicious recipes.

He was just *gone,* and his helpers started to worry. They had heard all about the contest between Santa and the Tooth Fairy. What if the Easter Bunny had now decided to take part?

With Easter just around the corner, work had to continue. But when they weren't cooking, wrapping or painting, every helper took turns to look for their friend and leader.

Martin had searched everywhere that he could think of, but there was no sign of the Easter Bunny and no clues to his disappearance. It was as if he had vanished into thin air!

In desperate need of a friendly face, he picked up the phone and dialled a number. Ben picked up after a couple of rings and listened closely as Martin explained the problem.

"That's awful!" he told his friend. "I'm really sorry to hear that, but I haven't seen the Easter Bunny here - the Tooth Fairy's been too busy to have visitors."

Martin's heart sank at the realisation of another dead end. "What about Santa?" he asked hopefully. "Do you think he might have gone to see him?"

"There's one way to find out," answered Ben, as he punched Luke's number into the communication screen. It rang for some time with no answer and Ben hung up.

"It doesn't look like there's anyone home, but that doesn't mean that we can't pay them a visit. I'll pick you up and we can head on over."

"How can you pick me up?" asked Martin. "Is someone giving you a lift?"

"I have wings now!" announced Ben, enjoying his friend's surprise. "It's a *very* long story – you won't believe everything that's been going on!"

***

Martin was indeed astounded to hear everything that had happened. The Easter Bunny's helpers knew all about the contest between Santa and the Tooth Fairy, but they hadn't realised how seriously both participants were taking it.

"It's pretty crazy," admitted Ben. "But we're all hoping that they'll see sense soon. After all, they can't keep going at this speed forever." He yawned and scratched his neck. "At least I hope not!"

When they arrived at Santa's home, the boys were surprised to find that there was no-one there to greet them. Normally some elves would be outside, laughing and giggling as they threw giant snowballs, or skiing and sledging over the crisp white snow.

But today the snow lay pristine and untouched, and the only noise to be heard was the faint braying of the reindeer inside their stalls.

"Come on," Ben urged his friend. "Let's go and see where everyone is."

Once inside it didn't take them long to track down the missing elves. The workshop was a hive of activity, with harassed looking elves running to and fro as they shouted instructions to each other.

The sound of banging and sawing echoed round the room. Some elves constructed handmade wooden toys, while others applied paint and decorations. Conveyer belts chugged and squeaked as they carried presents towards the workers who would wrap and decorate them.

Martin and Ben scanned the room for Luke, mumbling apologies to the elves who rushed past without stopping to acknowledge them.

"This is crazy!" marvelled Martin. "It's like someone's put them all on fast forward."

They eventually spotted Luke in the corner of the room. He was supervising a team of elves who were wrapping presents, barely having time to tie the final bow before yet another gift dropped down to join the waiting pile.

Luke gave a tired smile when he spotted them. He pulled out his whistle and blew it long and loud, causing everyone in the room to pause their tasks and wearily turn towards him.

"I think we could all do with a break," he announced. "I'll see you back here in half an hour."

The exhausted looking elves shuffled out of the room and Luke trudged over to meet his friends.

"Sorry about the chaos," he yawned. "It's been crazy here since Santa increased his deliveries. We've all been working nonstop to keep up."

His tired eyes began to close and his head began to droop. "Design toys... make toys... wrap toys..." he muttered sleepily.

Ben grabbed him by the shoulder and shook him vigorously. "Wake up, Luke! We need your help!"

With a tremendous effort, Luke raised his tired head. His eyes were barely open and he let out a massive yawn.

"I need a hot chocolate," he groaned. "Then we can talk."

***

Luke handed out the steaming mugs of hot chocolate

and the three friends sipped them as they talked. They were sat around the kitchen's oak dining table, with Luke starting to perk up as the tasty drink took effect.

Unfortunately, he couldn't shed any light on the Easter Bunny's disappearance.

"I haven't seen him since the party," he told his friends. "I'm sure that he's fine – maybe he just wants a little holiday before the Easter preparations ramp up."

"Maybe..." replied Martin, although that didn't sound like the Easter Bunny at all. Easter was his favourite time of year and he worked harder than anyone. "I just wish he'd give me a sign. I'm worried about him."

Before Luke and Ben could further reassure their friend, a loud banging noise filled the room. Curious, the boys stood up and began to walk around the kitchen, attempting to trace the noise to its source. They quickly realised that it seemed to be coming from behind an unassuming wooden door.

"Do you guys hear that?" asked Martin. "What's behind there?"

"That's the food store cupboard," Luke told him. "There's nothing in there that should make any noise."

"Not unless you have some *really* big mice at the North Pole," suggested Ben.

As if growing impatient with their debate, the banging grew louder, coupled with what appeared to be strange grunting noises.

Signalling his friends to be ready, Luke grabbed the handle and pulled the door open, revealing a most unexpected sight.

The Easter Bunny sat at the back of the store cupboard, almost entirely covered in wrapping paper and ribbons. His feet were bound together and most of his face was covered, barring his dark green eyes and his long ears.

Martin ran forward in a panic and began ripping paper off as fast as he could. "I thought you told me you hadn't seen him!" he snapped at Luke.

"I hadn't!" Luke protested. "I've no idea what he's doing here!"

Martin tore off the last strips of wrapping paper and

helped the Easter Bunny to his feet. The rescued rabbit stretched and flexed as he tried to get some feeling back into his numb limbs, moaning with pleasure.

"Don't blame Luke," he told Martin. "I'm afraid that Santa and I had a little disagreement."

Luke's eyes boggled. "Santa tied you up?" he spluttered. "He'd never do that – that's naughty list behaviour!"

The Easter Bunny placed a hairy paw on Luke's shoulder and smiled kindly. "Not normally, no. But Santa's been working hard lately and I think it's starting to get to him."

"It's this silly contest," complained Ben. "Does it really matter who does what as long as kids are happy?"

"Not really," answered Martin. "If only both of them could see how hard the other one works."

The Easter Bunny let out a joyous laugh and began to bounce around the room, jumping over tables and chairs and pirouetting off the walls.

"That's it! I think you've cracked this!"

"I have?" asked Martin. "What did I say?"

The Easter Bunny smiled and tapped his nose. "First, let's see if we can get Santa and Adora to come here. Then I think I've got a plan that will settle this contest once and for all!"

13

A CHANGE IS AS GOOD AS A REST

Santa closed the heavy stable door and let out an ear-popping yawn. It had been a long night, but all the hard work had been worth it. He had managed to deliver thousands more presents. That would show the Tooth Fairy who worked the hardest!

Deciding that his efforts had earned him a nice hot chocolate before bed, Santa strolled through the kitchen, singing happily to himself.

"Oh you better watch out, you better not cry
You better be good I'm telling you why.
Santa Claus is co- "

"AHEM!"

Santa spun round and the words died in his throat when he saw the small group assembled in the kitchen. Luke, Ben, Adora and Martin were all sat around the table, staring at him expectantly.

"Luke, what is *she* doing here?" Santa exclaimed. "What's going on?"

"I can answer that, Santa," said the Easter Bunny as he stepped into view.

Santa looked at him guiltily, his face turning almost as red as his suit. "Ah, Bunny, my old friend. I'm dreadfully sorry about earlier – I don't know what I was thinking!"

"I know *exactly* what you were thinking," replied the Easter Bunny, crossing his arms and giving Santa a disapproving look. "About this silly contest and how to win it."

"She started it!" protested Santa, pointing an accusing finger at the Tooth Fairy.

"I did not!" Adora shouted. "You did with all your boasting at the party!"

They continued to argue back and forward, with neither one willing to listen to the other. Luke, Ben and Martin looked at each other in despair.

"QUIET!!!!!!!!!!!!!!!!!!"

The Easter Bunny sighed in exasperation. "You're both behaving like children! You certainly aren't acting like you're hundreds of years old."

He pulled out a chair and beckoned for Santa to sit down. Santa grudgingly did so, purposely angling his chair so that he wasn't facing Adora.

The Easter Bunny gestured towards Martin, Luke and Ben. "I don't think the pair of you realise what this contest is doing to the people you care about! You're working your helpers so hard that they're exhausted."

"They haven't said anything," Santa argued.

"That's because you haven't asked!" the Easter Bunny admonished him. "You've been so wrapped up in proving a point to Adora that you haven't thought about anyone else."

Santa tutted dismissively, but his eyes widened in shock when he saw Luke. It had only been a matter of days since he had seen him, but the change in Luke's appearance was stark. He looked tired and stressed, with large bags visible under his eyes.

"My boy," Santa exclaimed, feeling a burst of gratitude for his helpers and all their hard work. "I'm so sorry!"

"That's okay, Santa," Luke smiled wearily. "Just please listen to the Easter Bunny – we really need to sort this."

"We certainly do!" said Adora, taking Ben's hand and giving it a friendly squeeze. "I'm just as much to blame – my helpers have been so busy these last few weeks."

The Easter Bunny clapped his paws together in delight. "Finally! I'm glad you both recognise that this can't go on."

Smiling broadly, he placed his paws on the table and leaned closer. "If you want to settle this contest once and for all, then I think I have the perfect idea..."

Adora and Santa looked at him curiously. Although both felt guilty for working their helpers so hard, neither of them wanted to be the first to concede defeat in their argument.

"Do you now?" Adora said, trying her best to appear uninterested. "What do you mean?"

The Easter Bunny gave a toothy grin, confident that he had their attention. His long whiskers quivered with excitement as he spoke.

"Neither of you will ever believe that the other one works harder. That's partly because you don't really know what the other's job involves."

He paused, letting the thought take root in his listeners' heads. Then, when he was sure that the seed was successfully planted, he continued.

"Both of you say how special your job is and that no-one else could do it, so I think there's only one way to put that to the test. *Swap jobs!*"

Santa gagged on a mouthful of hot chocolate, coughing and spluttering as it went down the wrong way.

"Swap jobs!" he exclaimed. "Ridiculous! Do you know how many presents I deliver? And why would I want to spend my nights picking up dirty old teeth?"

Adora glared at Santa, annoyed with his rudeness. "I'm not sure you could cope with my job – do you even visit houses if they don't leave out food for you?"

Their bickering continued and the weary helpers looked imploringly at the Easter Bunny, hoping that he could help calm things down.

RAT TAT TAT!

The sound of the Easter Bunny banging a carrot off the table surface helped break up the argument. Reluctantly, Santa and Adora sat back down in their chairs, waiting to hear what their friend would say.

"I really am very sorry," apologised the Easter Bunny. "I didn't mean to cause another argument between you both. Of *course* you don't have to swap jobs – not if you think it would be too hard for you!"

As he said this, he gave Luke, Ben and Martin an exaggerated wink. The boys exchanged knowing glances as they realised what he was trying to do.

"Too hard!" laughed Adora. "I don't think so! The thought of being a passenger while someone else flies sounds lovely."

"And collecting teeth sounds like a dawdle!" boomed Santa. "Why, by the time I'm finished I bet there will be hundreds of songs about the Tooth Fairy!"

"That's the spirit!" encouraged the Easter Bunny as he hugged his friends. "Just you wait – this will allow you to walk in the other's shoes."

"Or stomp about in their silly boots," muttered Adora under her breath.

"I *do* think we should agree some rules," declared the Easter Bunny, producing a rolled-up piece of paper with a flourish. "And I just happen to have composed some earlier!" He unfurled the paper on the table and beckoned everyone round. "Have a read and see what you think!"

We, the undersigned, do agree to swap jobs for the period of one week. The conditions of the swap are as follows:

1. *Participants will, as far as possible, emulate the look and role of their opposite number.*
2. *Participants will carry out all tasks to the best of their ability.*
3. *Participants are entitled to any help normally supplied to their opposite number. This includes transport, helpers and raw materials.*

4. *To ensure a fair contest, duties will seek to emulate 'normal' job roles. Therefore, the participant taking on duties of 'The Tooth Fairy' will only leave coins. The participant taking on duties of 'Santa Claus' will leave ONE present per child.*

5. *Visits should be carried out at night-time, while children are asleep.*

"I suppose one week isn't too long," mused Adora.

"Absolutely!" boomed Santa. "It'll be like a holiday!"

The Easter Bunny beamed and passed them both a jet-black fountain pen that he had produced from his bountiful pockets.

"Marvellous! Then let's sign here and make it official!"

Santa and Adora took turns at signing their names, both feeling considerably more apprehensive than they were letting on.

"So, this job swap," asked Santa. "When is it going to start?"

"How about now?" suggested the Easter Bunny. "There's no time like the present!"

He ushered Santa and Adora to one side and the three of them began to thrash out details. Their helpers exchanged glances as they watched them, unsure whether this swap would turn out to be a good idea or a VERY bad one.

14

MEET THE NEW BOSS

"I look ridiculous!" complained Santa as he peered at the unfamiliar reflection in the mirror.

The elegant pink dress may have looked wonderful on the Tooth Fairy, but Santa couldn't carry off the look nearly as well. Even with the dress being altered to accommodate his increased height and ample stomach, it still looked like it had been shrunk in a hot wash.

The dress reached down to just above Santa's knees, exposing chunky legs covered with thick black hairs that curled out like springs. Santa's choice of footwear made his outfit look even stranger. Instead of copying the Tooth Fairy's smart shoes he was still wearing his ancient black boots, having point-blank refused to wear anything else.

"I'm sure it will look better when you're fully dressed," Ben reassured him, stretching to place the gleaming gold tiara on Santa's head. It took several attempts before he could get it to remain in position on Santa's unkempt hair, and even then it tipped markedly to one side.

Ben stood back and surveyed his handiwork. Looking at the strange sight before him, he wasn't quite sure whether to laugh or cry.

"EEEEEEEEEEEEEK!"

A fairy imp chose just the wrong time to enter the room, and its eyes widened in horror as it took in Santa's new look.

Santa gave the imp a friendly wave, exposing a *very* hairy armpit.

"Hello, little one!" he called. "How do I look?"

The fairy imp didn't stick around to answer. Instead

it turned on its heels and flew away screaming, trying to get as far away from the disturbing sight as possible.

Santa sighed and scuffed his boots together. "This is a terrible idea," he grumbled. "Do I really need to dress like this?"

"You remember what you agreed with the Easter Bunny," Ben chided him. "You both said that you would emulate the 'look and role' of the other."

"Fine, if I must," pouted Santa. "But I'm NOT shaving my legs."

Ben shuddered, trying to push the disturbing mental image out of his head.

"That's okay, no shaving required." Ben looked at Santa hopefully as a thought occurred to him. "Unless you'd like to shave your beard off?"

Santa raised one eyebrow. Nothing more needed to be said.

"It was worth a try," said Ben. "Come on, let's give you the grand tour."

***

"You really like teeth here, don't you?"

Ben led Santa through the Tooth Fairy's castle, trying to ignore the accusing glares of the fairy imps. His friends were outraged that their beloved Tooth Fairy had been replaced, but luckily Santa was too busy taking in the sights to notice.

He stopped before the tooth polishing machine and examined it closely. It was chugging and whirring away as it cleaned a new batch of teeth, removing stains and dirt and spitting them out in pristine condition.

"I can see why you need this contraption," Santa said. "Teeth certainly look better when they're clean."

"Just don't get too close," warned Ben, speaking from bitter experience. "There's such a thing as being *too* clean."

"What's so interesting about teeth anyway?" asked Santa as he picked up a freshly polished tooth and examined it closely. "Aren't they a bit boring?"

The noise and bustle of the castle instantly stopped, as if someone had flicked a switch. As the tooth polishing machine came to the end of its cycle and its motors slowed, there was a deathly silence.

Ben and Santa slowly turned around to find hundreds of fairy imps hovering in mid-air, glaring at them. Some were frowning, with their arms folded tightly across their chests. Others stuck their tongues out and pulled cheeky faces.

"I think you've upset them," Santa whispered to Ben.

"*I've* upset them?" spluttered Ben. "*You* need to talk to them and get them on your side."

Ignoring Santa's protests, he pushed him forward into the full glare of the imps' disapproval.

"Hello fairy..." Santa paused and turned to Ben. "What are they called again?" he whispered.

"Fairy imps," Ben hissed.

"Hello fairy chimps!" called Santa.

There was a deafening chorus of boos and raspberries. Small fists were waved in the air and accusing fingers were jabbed in Santa's direction.

"Fairy IMPS!" shouted Ben.

"Ah, fairy imps. My apologies! Thank you for inviting

me into your lovely home. I know it must feel strange not to have Adora here, but I promise that I'm going to work hard."

The murmurs of disapproval began to die down. The fairy imps were interested in what Santa had to say, wanting to know what was coming next.

"Ben here is just making sure that I'm all prepared, then I promise that I'll bring back all the teeth you could possibly want!"

Santa smiled as the fairy imps cheered and whooped, happy that he'd managed to win them over.

"And then we'll all celebrate with some lovely hot chocolate!"

The cheering died down as quickly as it had started, leaving Santa unsure what had happened. "What did I say?" he asked Ben.

"We don't have hot chocolate here – or any chocolate at all," Ben replied. "It's bad for your teeth, you know."

Santa turned pale, holding on to the tooth polishing machine for support.

"This is going to be the longest week of my life," he moaned.

***

Ben soared through the air, twisting to squeeze his body through the silver hoop that hung down from the ceiling. He zigzagged between the plastic poles embedded in the floor, before shooting upwards and pressing the red button that was located near the top of the wall.

There was a series of shrill beeps and the obstacles began to reset themselves, retreating out of sight. Delighted at his performance, Ben flew down to join the watching Santa, who was looking less than convinced.

"See! It's simple if you just give it a try."

"I must have been mad to agree to this," muttered Santa as he adjusted the straps of his harness. Like Ben, Santa had been given a set of mechanical wings. Although he had agreed to try them on, getting him to use them was another matter entirely.

"Just give it a try," coaxed Ben. "You don't have to do anything fancy the first time – just float into the air and then straight back down again."

"That sounds doable," agreed Santa. "Straight up and straight down."

With a look of intense concentration on his face, he set the wings in motion and began to slowly rise into the air.

"I'm doing it!" he chortled in delight. "Ben, my boy – I'm doing it!"

"That's great, Santa," replied Ben. "Just stay focused."

A small group of fairy imps had gathered at the door and were watching Santa's progress with interest. Their whispers and giggles made it clear that they weren't anticipating success.

It initially seemed that they would be disappointed. Santa rose into the air somewhat erratically, but successfully enough to overcome his initial hesitance.

Which is when it all went wrong.

With his confidence growing, Santa decided to try

some more advanced flying moves. He'd seen his reindeer whiz through the air often enough – surely he could do the same?

Santa quickly found that although he was big and hairy, he was no reindeer.

He tried to turn to the left but went too far, causing him to spin in circles like a hairy spinning top. Growing dizzier by the second, he tried to fly in the opposite direction but overcompensated, sending him flying across the room.

"WOOAAAAAHHHH!"

The watching fairy imps ducked as Santa hurtled over their heads, turning head over heels as he spun around the room. They laughed hysterically as they watched Ben run after Santa, enjoying the unexpected entertainment.

"SANTA, STOP FLYING!" shouted Ben, as he watched Santa ricochet around the room like a hyperactive pinball.

"I can't stop!" shouted Santa, as he flew backwards at increasing speed. "HELP!"

Ben frantically looked around the room, searching for inspiration. The fairy imps were no use - they were collapsed on the floor with tears of laughter running down their cheeks. And there was no way that Santa could stop himself.

Then Ben had an idea.

He pressed the power button on the control panel and the room's obstacles gradually came into view. Long poles emerged from the floor and the silver hoop descended from the ceiling.

Santa managed to avoid the first and second poles but clipped the third one at speed, sending him spinning into the air. He collided with the hoop and lurched forwards so that he was hanging downwards, suspended in position by his heavy boots.

The fairy imps began to clamber to their feet, glaring at Ben for spoiling their fun. Then gravity took its toll. Santa's dress turned inside out and fell over his head, revealing the furry red knickers he was wearing.

The fairy imps practically exploded with glee, almost wetting themselves with laughter as they rolled about the floor, clutching their aching sides.

"Hello," called Santa. "Is anyone there? How did I do?"

"You were brilliant," Ben lied, trying his best not to look at Santa's pants. "You're a natural."

"Excellent. Then let's go and collect some teeth!"

15

MINCE PIE MELTDOWN

The fairy imps weren't the only ones adjusting to some unexpected changes. At the North Pole, Luke led the Tooth Fairy through Santa's grotto, doing his best to highlight all the important details.

The task was made more difficult by the fact that Adora kept stopping to talk to every elf that she passed, introducing herself with a smile and a friendly greeting. The elves had grumbled and groaned when the job swap was first announced, but even the surliest worker found it hard to resist Adora's friendly nature.

Luke stood and watched as Adora chatted with

Bromly, her hand resting on his shoulder as they laughed at a shared joke. In her natural form, Adora was the same height as the elves, and she was obviously enjoying being around people her own size.

Luke eventually managed to extract her from the conversation and they continued towards the workshop, leaving Bromly waving enthusiastically at Adora's retreating form.

"Everyone here is so friendly," Adora smiled. "I can see why Santa likes it so much."

Luke beamed with pride, delighted that they had already managed to make such a favourable impression. "If you think that's impressive, wait until you see this!"

He opened the door to the workshop and ushered Adora through, unable to resist smiling at her awestruck reaction.

Adora had visited the North Pole many times, but normally for social occasions. Seeing the workshop in full flow – alive with noise, bustle and energy – was something else entirely.

The two of them stood in silence for a moment,

taking in the fantastical tableau before them. Although some elves called out greetings or gave a quick wave, they never lost their focus on the task in front of them. Whether building, decorating or packaging, it was obvious that each worker took pride in producing presents of the highest quality.

"My goodness," breathed Adora. "Look at them go – their fingers are almost blurs!"

She grabbed Luke's arm, squeezing it in excitement as she pointed across the room. "Look at how fast he's tying these bows!" she exclaimed in delight. "If I tried that I'd tie myself in knots!"

"He's had plenty of practice," smiled Luke. "We all have. One of the first things that Santa tells every new worker is that each toy is special. Whether they're given to a child who owns one toy or a hundred, they should all be made with the same care and attention."

Adora stood in silence for a time, a thoughtful expression on her face as she watched the activity within the room.

"I hope you know that I'm going to do my best," she told Luke. "Not just for this competition, but because I know how important this is to all of you."

"I know," Luke reassured her. "Let's finish the tour and you'll get a better idea what's in store for you."

***

"I'm sorry, but I just can't do it," protested Adora, resting her elbows on the kitchen table and running her fingers though her hair in frustration.

"You can," urged Luke, willing her on. "I believe in you!"

With an anguished moan, Adora picked up the mince pie and took a bite, dropping more crumbs onto the sizeable pile in front of her. Then she lifted a large tumbler of milk and took a hearty swig before swallowing it down.

"That's enough," she croaked as she wiped away the milk moustache with the back of her hand. "Please! 27 mince pies are all I can manage!"

"Okay," agreed Luke, taking pity on her. "But it is important that you work on your power eating. You've no idea how many of those things Santa has to eat in one night."

"I hate to think," replied Adora, who was now looking *very* queasy. As if worried that Luke would change his mind, she pushed the plate to one side and hurriedly stood up.

"So," she announced, keen to steer the subject away from food. "What now?"

Five minutes later, Adora was stood in the stables, holding her nose tightly and beginning to wish that she'd never asked.

"Are you sure that I have to wear this?" she asked Luke as she pushed up the long sleeves of Santa's coat for what felt like the hundredth time. "My normal colour is pink, not red."

She fanned her face and tugged at the thick material around her neck. "How does Santa put up with this every day? It's like wearing an electric blanket!"

"Santa has a very... individual dress sense," replied Luke. "But there is actually a good reason why I think you should wear it."

"Let me guess," replied Adora. "Because every child knows that Santa wears a red and white suit."

"That's a good guess, but I was thinking about a

more practical reason," smiled Luke. "Take off the jacket and I'll show you," he said, holding out his hand.

Unsure what to expect, Adora took off the thick jacket and handed it over, glad for a temporary reprieve from its stifling heat.

"Go and talk to the reindeer," Luke suggested, and Adora couldn't help noticing that he took a step backwards as he did so.

She walked hesitantly towards the stalls, the pungent smell growing stronger with every step. As she drew closer the noise from the stalls intensified and she could hear the scraping of hooves and distressed sounding grunts.

"Hello!" Adora called. "Nice to see you all again. I'm sorry that I haven't got any food for you."

CRASH!

Adora jumped backwards in shock as the agitated reindeer careered around their stalls, rising on their hindlegs and scraping their hooves against the stall door. Unnerved by this hostile reception, she hurried back towards Luke.

"What's the matter with them?" she asked. "Are they

sick? Are they hungry?"

"Put on the jacket and you'll see," said Luke, handing it back to her and smiling encouragingly.

Adora was by no means certain that she wanted to tempt fate by visiting the reindeer for a second time. But, gathering her courage, she reluctantly made her way towards their stalls.

"Hello," she whispered, terrified of startling them. "It's me again. I'm really nice – honest!"

Adora closed her eyes tight, expecting the worst. But then, as if in response to her plea, Rudolph and Dancer trotted over. They bent their majestic heads over the stall door and began snuffling Adora, licking her face all over with their rough tongues.

Adora was taken aback by the sudden transformation, and her laugh was a mixture of surprise, delight and sheer relief. "What happened?" she asked Luke. "I thought they didn't like me?"

"It's the outfit," Luke told her. "They only behave for Santa, and with that on you're the closest thing we've got."

He reached out to pat Rudolph and then thought

better of it, drawing his hand back as the reindeer snorted at him. "You'll be doing us all a big favour if you keep wearing that. If not, feeding time could be quite hazardous..."

Adora scratched Rudolph's scalp and he emitted a grunt of pleasure that caught the attention of his friends. Soon, all nine reindeer were crowded around Adora, jostling for position and desperate to attract her attention.

"You're all such good boys," she chuckled. "Tell me, how would you feel about helping me with some deliveries?"

16

TOOTH FAIRY IN TRAINING

At helper orientation the Tooth Fairy always broke her visit routine into three simple steps.

1. A child leaves a tooth out for collection, normally under a pillow

2. The Tooth Fairy collects the tooth.

3. The Tooth Fairy leaves money in exchange for the tooth.

Collect the tooth and leave money – that seemed a simple process to Ben, something that adults and children alike could easily grasp.

So why was Santa making him tear his hair out in

frustration?

The evening had started off well. Despite his less than impressive start, Santa had quickly mastered his wings and was enjoying flying through the air. He seemed full of enthusiasm for the night ahead, determined to prove that he could easily do the Tooth Fairy's job.

When they reached the first house they had paused outside while Ben gave Santa a final pep talk.

"Now, you're absolutely sure that you don't want me to come inside with you?" Ben asked.

"There's no need," said Santa. "I've been doing home visits for a long time, so I'm a bit of an expert!"

Ben crossed his fingers behind his back, hoping that Santa was as good as he claimed. "Okay, let's run over the routine one more time."

"If we must," Santa sighed. "I teleport myself into the house; I take the tooth from under the pillow; I leave money and then I teleport myself out again."

He raised an eyebrow and gave Ben a challenging look. "I think that should be everything?"

Ben wracked his brains, trying to think of anything that Santa had missed, but it did seem like he had thought of everything.

"Okay," he said, swallowing nervously. "You can go in."

Santa tapped his nose and vanished, leaving Ben anxiously pacing back and forward on the roof. In less than a minute, Santa reappeared, looking *very* pleased with himself.

"It went okay?" Ben asked him, desperate for reassurance. "You didn't wake up the child, or knock over a bookcase, or- "

"It went fine," replied Santa. "I even saved us some money!"

Santa opened his palm to reveal both the tooth and a shiny £1 coin, giving Ben heart palpitations.

"You didn't leave money!" he shouted, grabbing the pound coin from Santa and waving it at him in disbelief. "You have to leave money! Collect the tooth and leave money! COLLECT THE TOOTH AND LEAVE MONEY!"

"Don't worry, I left him something," replied Santa,

retrieving the pound coin and carefully placing it back in the bag. "I know the rules – we take the tooth and leave something behind."

"Then what did you leave him?" asked Ben, beginning to wonder if Santa and the Tooth Fairy were playing an elaborate prank on him.

"A lump of coal," answered Santa. "Tucked right under his pillow."

Ben blinked in confusion, trying to process what he'd just heard.

"You... left him *coal?*"

"That's right!"

"Under his *pillow?*"

"Tucked in all snug!"

"You left **coal** for a **tooth?**"

Ben tried to say more, but he was so gobsmacked that he was tongue-tied, quite unable to make any sound apart from strange grunting noises.

"I did," Santa answered proudly. He held out the tooth for Ben to see, pointing to the tiny hole in the side and the yellow staining around the edges.

"It's utterly filthy," he told Ben, "and the boy obviously never took good care of it. His lump of coal is well deserved!"

He slipped the tooth into his bag and stepped forward to the edge of the roof. "Race you to the next house!" he called.

"Santa, hold on a second!" Ben blurted out, finally finding his voice. "You can't leave coal on a visit."

Santa turned back, looking puzzled. "But it was *filthy*," he explained. "We don't *reward* that, do we?"

"I know it's different from what you're used to, but the Tooth Fairy treats every child the same. It doesn't matter what condition their teeth are in; every child gets some money."

"All of them?" exclaimed Santa. "Well I never!"

***

Later that night, Ben found out that Santa had taken his advice rather too literally. They had visited ten houses, and Santa appeared to be settling into a nice routine.

Just in case, Ben made sure to remind him to 'Collect the tooth and leave money' every time.

When Santa reappeared with the tooth in his possession, he showed it to Ben, pointing out what good condition it was in.

"Look how white it is – there's hardly a mark on it. It's definitely worthy of the top rate!"

He placed the tooth into his bag and the two were just about to leave for their next destination when a disturbing thought struck Ben.

"Santa, you said 'Worthy of the top rate'. What did you mean?"

Santa chuckled. "Only that it was definitely deserving of £1. Not like some of those *other* teeth!"

Ben felt his stomach flip and he had to force himself to ask the question, certain that he wouldn't like the answer he'd receive.

"Other teeth? What do you mean?"

"The other teeth we've collected, of course! There haven't been many to warrant £1 tonight. We've had some covered in dirt, some covered in blood, and some have been absolutely *tiny*. That girl at the third house was lucky to get ten pence, believe me! I must be feeling generous tonight!"

Santa gave a hearty laugh which tailed off as he realised that Ben wasn't sharing his amusement. Ben had an expression of quiet despair on his face, looking like he was about to burst into tears.

"You've given everyone *different money*," he announced in an anguished moan.

"Yes..." replied Santa. "Is that a problem?"

Ben stared down at his feet, clenching and unclenching his fists. When he eventually raised his head, he looked completely exhausted. "Okay, new plan," he sighed. "We start the visits again, from the beginning, and this time EVERYBODY gets the *same amount* of money. No lumps of coal, no different amounts, everyone gets the same!"

"Right. Brilliant," agreed Santa. "Just one question – can we leave IOUs?"

"I don't know how the reindeer put up with him," Ben muttered under his breath.

***

The fifteenth visit of the night brought Santa and Ben to the Scottish Highlands, to a house in the small village of Inchmore. The two of them hovered outside the front bedroom window while Ben ran through the pre-visit checklist, satisfying himself that Santa was clear on what to do.

"Stop fussing," Santa protested. "I know what to do by now!" Before Ben could reply, Santa tapped his nose and vanished, instantly appearing within the sleeping child's bedroom.

"Collect the tooth and leave money," Santa muttered to himself as he tiptoed towards the bed. "Collect the tooth and leave money."

The sleeping girl was breathing softly as she lay on her back, holding on tightly to a bright pink stuffed unicorn.

"Don't get any ideas," Santa told the toy, eyeing it warily.

Something about the sleeping child looked familiar,

and Santa chuckled to himself as he realised who she was. "Dora Evans!" he exclaimed. "I gave you the PJ Masks HQ for Christmas – I hope that you like it."

He began to wander around the room, searching for the present among the countless toys that filled every available space. Unfortunately, Santa was so caught up in his search that he didn't notice a dark shape on the floor by the bed; not until he walked into it, kicking it with his heavy black boot.

"OW!" the shape shouted, before rising unsteadily to its feet. An arm reached towards the nightlight, fumbling for the switch, and the bulb lit up to reveal Mrs Evans, who had fallen asleep on the floor while comforting her upset daughter.

It would have been a simple task for Santa to teleport out of the room, but he was like a deer in headlights. The unexpected development had taken him totally by surprise.

Rubbing her tired eyes, Mrs Evans noticed for the first time that there was another figure within the room. Her eyes grew wide and she snapped fully awake as she took in the strange sight before her.

An elderly man was standing there, with an unkempt bushy beard and curly white hair, upon which sat a golden tiara. He was wearing a pink dress that was far too small for him, exposing hairy legs that led down to heavy black boots.

It was a sight so strange, so unexpected, that Mrs Evans could only muster one response.

"AAAAAAAAAAARRRRRRRRRRRRRRRGGGGG GGGGGGGGGHHHHHHHHHHHHH," she screamed, grabbing soft toys from the bed and throwing them at Santa. **"HELP!"**

Santa rocked backwards as a bright orange duck bounced off his nose, trying to evade the barrage of fluffy cuteness that rained down around him.

"You don't understand!" he shouted. "I'm only here for Dora!"

Mrs Evans gave an outraged shriek and placed herself between Santa and the bed. Having exhausted her supply of soft toys, she now resorted to throwing anything that was to hand. Books, toys and more were all sent hurtling in Santa's direction, forcing him to dive for cover.

Mrs Evans' grasping fingers closed around the hard-plastic nightlight, and without thinking she lifted it up and threw it towards Santa. Fortunately for Santa's skull, the power cord saved him from serious injury. It pulled taut when the light was halfway across the room, dropping the light to the floor and pulling the plug partially from the socket.

The room plunged into darkness and Santa saw his chance. Tapping his nose, he teleported behind Mrs Evans and over to the pillow, where he quickly pulled out the tooth and replaced it with a £1 coin. Then, tapping his nose again, he vanished from the room and appeared outside, next to the waiting Ben.

"You were in there for a long time," Ben told him. "Did everything go okay?"

"That depends. What did you hear?"

"Nothing," Ben replied, giving him a quizzical look. "Is there something that you'd like to tell me?"

"No, definitely not," Santa assured him. "Come on,

we better get a move on."

The two of them flew into the night sky, Santa sneaking guilty looks at the lights that flickered on in the Evans household.

17

FAIRY CLAUS IS COMING TO TOWN

Adora was *not* in a good mood.

Despite all her preparation and good intentions, the night hadn't gone as smoothly as she'd hoped. It had taken Adora and Luke twenty minutes to locate the first present within the cavernous interior of Santa's sack, putting them immediately behind schedule. And while landing the sleigh on flat roofs had proved no problem, slanted roofs were rather trickier.

None of these things were Adora's fault – after all, Santa had perfected his technique over millions of visits. But she was so anxious to impress that she grew increasingly frustrated with each new setback.

Which is why her discovery on the fifth visit made her so very *annoyed*.

The bedrooms on the first and second visits had no drink or snack laid out, but Adora was so focused on delivering the correct present that she barely noticed. There was nothing on the third or fourth visits either, but Adora didn't think much of it. But when there was nothing left out on the fifth visit, she began to wonder what was going on.

"There was no drink or biscuit," she complained to Luke when she returned to the sleigh. "I'm absolutely starving!"

Luke looked puzzled, but this was quickly replaced by a look of acute embarrassment as he blushed bright red.

"Ah, I *think* I may know why that is," he explained. "You see, I'm used to planning for deliveries on Christmas Eve, when everyone knows that Santa is coming. And tonight... well, no-one knows that he – by which I mean you, I guess - is coming."

Adora stared at him in disbelief as the full realisation

of his words sank in. "27 mince pies! You made me eat 27 mince pies for *nothing*!"

She placed a hand over her belly, giving it an apologetic pat. "It's a good thing that these trousers are elasticated, because I probably won't fit into my dress anymore!"

***

Later that night, Adora listened carefully as Luke set out the details of the next visit.

"There are twin brothers in this house – Ethan and Adam Beswick. They're aged 10 years old."

"Two visits at once," smiled Adora, clapping her hands together with glee. "That'll help us to get back on track! Let's see what we've got for them tonight."

Adora opened the sack and rummaged inside, before producing two presents that could not have been more different.

One was wrapped in thick, glossy paper, the edges beautifully folded and sellotaped. A magnificent silver ribbon adorned the top, tied in a bow with more loops than a giant rollercoaster.

The other present was a lump of coal.

Adora turned it over to examine it, wondering if it was actually some kind of Transformer. But when she saw the black dust left on her fingers, she realised that it was what it seemed.

Not a soft toy coal or a coal science kit. An *actual* lump of coal!

"There must be some mistake," she told Luke. "Ethan's got a present, but all Adam has is a lump of coal."

"No mistake," said Luke. "Adam's on the naughty list, so he's only getting coal this year. He plays the naughtiest practical jokes on his brother."

"But you can't just give him coal!" Adora spluttered. "Especially not when his brother is getting a present. That's not fair!"

Luke shrugged. "He's on the naughty list. If he wanted a present from Santa then he should have been nice – children know the rules."

Adora threw the lump of coal to the floor and placed her hands on her hips, glaring daggers at Luke and making her disapproval clear. "Well *I* say that it's not right. All children should be treated the same."

"But that's not how it works," pleaded Luke. "That's not how Santa does it."

"Well it's how *I'm* going to do it," announced Adora. "And right now, I'm the boss!"

She reached into the bag and pulled out a present at random, examining the name on the tag. "Robin Jarvis – is he due to get a present tonight?"

Luke flicked through the pages of his list, looking increasingly worried. "No, but- "

"No buts!" said Adora. "Adam deserves a present and he's getting one. Take a note to replace Robin's present when we get back."

Adora reached out and grabbed Luke's pen from him, scoring out Robin Jarvis and replacing it with Adam Beswick. "There!" she announced. "It's not the tidiest but it will do. And when we get back to the North Pole that naughty list is going straight in the bin!"

She grabbed the two presents and used her wand to summon the golden light, its shimmering aura carrying her through the air and into the bedroom. Luke watched her go, feeling sick with worry. Adora was just joking about the naughty list, wasn't she?

He absentmindedly reached out to stroke Cupid, but the huge reindeer grunted in irritation and shook him off. Luke sank back in his seat and gazed up at the stars that littered the inky sky. Santa was somewhere out there, making visits of his own.

"I wish you would come back home," Luke whispered.

18

MY WAY OR THE HIGHWAY

Luke quickly found that Adora hadn't been joking.

Her first act upon their return to the North Pole was to summon all the elves together for an emergency meeting.

It was early in the morning, that small period between night owls succumbing to slumber and early risers springing out of bed. The elves stumbled through in dribs and drabs, yawning and in various stages of undress.

Some had pulled on the nearest clothes to hand, their mismatched outfits and zany bedhead making them look like walking scarecrows. Others had simply stayed in their pyjamas, stifling yawns as they waited to hear what news was important enough to warrant a 4am wake-up call.

The elves stared up at Luke as he stood beside Adora on the stage, as if expecting him to provide some sort of clue. All he could do was shrug his shoulders; he was as much in the dark as anyone.

When Adora was satisfied that all the elves were present, she tapped her wand on the edge of the lectern to get their attention.

"Thank you all for coming," she told the gathered crowd. "I know that it's very early, but this really couldn't wait."

She absentmindedly tapped the head of her wand in the palm of her hand as she walked about the stage, choosing her next words carefully.

"I've learnt a lot tonight," she said. "It's clear to me how hard Santa works and how much children love his visits."

The elves exchanged smiles, pleased to hear Adora praising Santa. Her next words weren't received quite

GARY SMITH

so warmly.

"That's why I am so *disappointed* with the way that Santa treats some children."

There were shocked gasps from the crowd and the elves wondered if they had misheard. What could she mean? Didn't children love Santa *because* of how well he treated them?

Adora waited for the noise to subside and then continued.

"Giving some children coal for Christmas is *not right*. When their brothers and sisters get presents; when all their friends at school get presents; how is it right that they only get coal?"

"Because they're on the naughty list," answered Bromly. "Children know what happens if they're bad."

"And who decides that they're naughty?" asked Adora. "I'm sure that everyone here has done something that they're embarrassed by or ashamed of. How would we feel if one silly moment meant that we ended up on the naughty list?"

Some elves exchanged furtive glances, sharing a guilty secret. Others looked at their feet, feeling embarrassed as they recalled past naughtiness. But their faith in Santa was absolute – if he had a naughty list then there must be a very good reason for it!

"I don't mean to be rude," Luke told her, "but you've only delivered presents for one night. Santa has been doing this for hundreds of years."

Adora bristled, her pride stung by his words. "I've been doing my *own* deliveries for hundreds of years! I know children and I know what's fair."

She reached into the deep pockets of Santa's suit and extracted the naughty list scroll, provoking awestruck gasps from the assembled elves.

"Be careful," pleaded Luke. "Santa will need that when he gets back."

"Well that's too bad," replied Adora. "This list is **wrong** and I'm not going to stand for it!"

She threw the scroll into the air, the paper unfurling to reveal the countless names recorded in Santa's spidery handwriting. Then Adora raised her wand and pointed.

There was a pregnant pause as time within the workshop seemed to stand still. It felt like every person in the room was holding their breath, waiting to see what would happen next. Then the naughty list was enveloped in a fiery glow, the heat growing in intensity until the scroll beneath was completely hidden from view.

When the colour faded, all that was left was a pile of ash that drifted down to the floor, scattering over the stage like dust in the wind.

The naughty list was **no more.**

UPROAR!

CHAOS!

Hysteria threatened to take hold of the room as the elves realised what had happened. Workers who only that morning had hung on Adora's every word now shouted protests and voiced their anger.

A chant went up from around the room, starting with scattered elves but soon taken up by all.

"SANTA! SANTA! SANTA!"

"This is for the best!" Adora pleaded, trying to regain control of her audience. "It wasn't fair to treat some children differently – don't you see?"

Egged on by his friends, Nedzil climbed on stage and jogged over to Adora until they were standing face to face.

"The only thing we see is someone trying to do a job that they're not up to," he shouted. "We're not going to help you undo all Santa's good work. That's why we're... we're..."

Nedzil tailed off, suddenly realising that he had no

idea how to proceed. Then a loud voice from the rear of the room shouted, **"WE'RE GOING ON STRIKE!"**

The voice sounded familiar and Luke craned his neck to identify the speaker, but all he saw was a brief glimpse of an elbow as the speaker hurried out the door.

"That's right!" agreed Nedzil, spurred into action. "We're going on strike. All of us!"

There was a brief pause as the elves digested the impact of his words. Work was all they knew – it was their life and their very reason for being. Yet perhaps only a strike would have the effect of bringing their beloved Santa back.

"STRIKE, STRIKE, STRIKE!" they chanted as Nedzil marched them towards the exit, with none even bothering to say farewell to Adora. She tried to call them back, to plead her case and explain her reasons. But in no time at all the room was empty, leaving Adora and Luke alone on the stage.

Adora slumped down on the floor, looking completely dejected as she surveyed the empty room. "They didn't even listen to me," she sighed. "I didn't do this to win some feud with Santa, I did it because it was the right thing to do!"

She jumped to her feet and ran over to Luke, grabbing his collar and pulling him close.

"You'll still help me, won't you? Please, Luke – I can't do this by myself!"

Luke was conflicted, unsure what to say. He was outraged at the destruction of the naughty list, but he couldn't help thinking back to the twins and Adora's concern for Adam's happiness.

He gave a big sigh, wondering when his life had become so *complicated*.

"I'll help you," he told her. "As long as you don't do anything like this again."

Adora wrapped her arms around him, squeezing him tight until he could barely breathe. "Oh, thank you, thank you, thank you! You won't regret this, I promise!"

Luke thought about his friends and how angry they had been. What would they say when they found out that he was still helping Adora?

"I hope you're right," he told her, crossing his fingers.

19

KARAOKE CALAMITY

The atmosphere at the Tooth Fairy's castle couldn't have been more different. Santa held the fairy imps spellbound as he recounted his night's work, and the imps cheered and whooped as he held up a large bag of teeth – the latest additions to the Tooth Fairy's collection.

With a showman's flourish, Santa poured out the teeth and the imps crowded round, fighting and jostling to get near.

Santa smiled broadly as he made his way through the crowds, waving and high fiving as he went. He stopped beside Ben and the two of them stood in silence for a moment, watching the festivities unfold.

"That was a rather successful first night," declared Santa, sounding very pleased with himself. "I think we all deserve a little reward."

"What did you have in mind?" asked Ben.

Santa grinned. "Tell me, have you ever sung Karaoke?"

***

Santa was in his element. Microphone in hand, he stood in front of the crowd and sang his heart out to all his favourite songs. Between numbers he told stories about his past adventures, recounting successful visits and daring escapades.

The fairy imps sat cross legged before him, wide-eyed and rapt with attention as they listened to Santa's embellished exploits.

Ben stood back and watched, unable to match the imps' enthusiasm. He was glad that Santa's first night had gone well, and was relieved that the fairy imps were beginning to accept him. But a small part of him couldn't help but feel *disappointed* that things were going so smoothly.

It wasn't because he disliked Santa; it was impossible to dislike someone so full of life and good cheer. It was just that it felt strange for them to be celebrating his success, as if they were somehow being disloyal to the Tooth Fairy.

The fairy imps cheered and clapped as Santa finished his party piece – an extended version of *Santa Claus is coming to town* that went on for fifteen minutes and included an improvised rap section.

"Thank you so much!" Santa beamed, bowing low and placing the microphone on the stage as he blew kisses towards the crowd. "I'm just going to get a little drink, then I'll be back for MORE SONGS!"

The room erupted with cheers and applause as Santa headed for the kitchen, Ben following behind.

Santa entered the kitchen and immediately began to rifle though cupboards, pawing aside tins and packets like a demented squirrel.

"I know what you're looking for," Ben told him. "I wasn't tricking you – there's no chocolate here."

Santa popped his head out of a cupboard, barely visible among the teetering piles of cereal boxes and tins of food that were scattered around him. "Well what do you have?" he asked. "What's the drink of choice for Adora and chums?"

Ben walked to the huge fridge and pulled the door open. Santa's mouth dropped open in amazement as he gazed at the hundreds of cartons that filled the fridge, lining every shelf.

"Milk!" smiled Ben as he poured Santa a glass. "Good for healthy bones and teeth!"

Santa took the glass and looked at it morosely. "I get enough of this stuff on my visits," he muttered.

Taking a hearty swig, he sat back in his chair and looked around him "This is some place you have here," he told Ben. "Certainly different from what I'm used to."

"Different in what way?"

"It smells better for one thing," chuckled Santa. "I love my reindeer, but even I have to admit that they can get quite whiffy at times!"

He shuffled about in his chair, rearranging his dress as he tried to get comfortable.

"You've all made me feel very welcome, but I have to admit that I'm still a little baffled by what you do here."

"How so?" asked Ben, coming to join him at the table. Caught up in their conversation, neither of them noticed the kitchen door open and a hand push the microphone through, its red light blinking rhythmically.

"All this effort for teeth! Did you see how excited the fairy imps got when I poured the bag out? I can't see the attraction myself."

"It's what we do here," Ben shrugged. "The Tooth Fairy probably thinks the same thing about the North Pole."

"I highly doubt it!" snorted Santa. "You should see some of the wonderful presents that we deliver. Now *they're* worth getting excited about. Not like some dirty old teeth!"

He chuckled to himself and took another drink.

Then, noticing the look of annoyance on Ben's golden features, Santa realised that perhaps he'd been a little tactless.

"I'm sorry, that was rude of me. The teeth look *very* nice once they're polished. And if Adora wants to spend all her time collecting them then that's lovely. After all, I can't see anyone else wanting them!"

Santa drained the last of his milk and placed the glass in the sink. "Come on, let's go see what my audience want to hear next. I have a few numbers that I've been dying to try out!"

Santa walked out to find a huge crowd of fairy imps waiting for him. But unlike earlier, they weren't smiling and in good cheer. They looked angry and upset, with some on the brink of tears.

"Were you coming to find me?" asked Santa, beaming with pleasure. "My goodness you are keen!"

"Santa, you should look at this." Ben tugged insistently at Santa's arm, holding the microphone that he had found by the door.

"My microphone! So, you want to hear me as well! I

knew that you were enjoying it really!"

"I found it in the kitchen," Ben told him, pointing at the flashing red light.

"The kitchen?"

Ben held the microphone to his mouth and spoke slowly and clearly, his every word amplified through the giant speakers. "I. FOUND. IT. IN. THE. KITCHEN!"

Santa looked between the microphone, the fairy imps and the speakers, realisation slowly dawning.

"Ah," he said, as the penny finally dropped.

The fairy imps didn't wait for an explanation. Blowing raspberries and chattering insults, they flew out of the room without looking back, leaving Ben and Santa alone.

"Stupid old fool," Santa rebuked himself, hitting his forehead in frustration. "Why do you never know when to keep your mouth shut?"

Santa continued to berate himself, but Ben wasn't listening. He was looking around the room, his forehead furrowed with concentration.

He was *sure* that he'd seen Santa place the

microphone on the stage after his song finished.

But if Santa hadn't brought the microphone to the kitchen, who had?

20

RETURN TO SENDER

"SHE DID WHAT?!" Ben shouted in disbelief. "You're pulling my leg!"

Luke pulled him back against the stable wall and held a finger to his lips, signalling him to be quiet. The two friends had met up to compare notes about recent disasters, desperate to find a solution that would return things to normal.

"Keep your voice down!" hissed Luke. "You don't want the elves to see you – they're not too keen on anything tooth related at the moment."

"They can't be as bad as the fairy imps," Ben told

him. "They haven't spoken to Santa for days. They've even hidden his Karaoke machine!"

Luke sighed and buried his face in his hands. "This is an absolute DISASTER! Swap jobs! Next time I see the Easter Bunny I'm going to tell him what a terrible idea that was!"

"Not if I tell him first," said Ben. "I just want things to go back to normal. It's not fun anymore."

"You've got that right," Luke agreed. "And I think we both know who's to blame for starting this whole mess."

"We certainly do," replied Ben.

"The Tooth Fairy," said Luke.

"Santa," said Ben.

The two friends looked at each other in surprise then both began talking at the same time, the words gushing out of them in a furious torrent.

"How can you possibly say that? It's obviously Santa's fault for being such a bighead!"

"Are you serious? Everyone saw Adora start an argument at the Christmas party."

"GAAARRROOOH!!!!!"

The agitated grunting from the reindeer pen halted Ben and Luke midargument. They looked at each other sheepishly, feeling slightly ashamed of losing their temper.

"I think they were *both* a little at fault to start with," said Ben. "But what made things really bad was when Santa wrote his letter to the Tooth Fairy. He- "

Ben tailed off as he noticed Luke staring at him strangely. "What is it now?" he grumbled in exasperation.

"You've said that before," Luke told him. "That Santa wrote the Tooth Fairy a letter. But that's not right – it was Adora that wrote to Santa!"

"Nope!" proclaimed Ben as he began to rummage through his pockets. After extracting snotty tissues, stones, feathers and some frayed elastic bands, he finally pulled out a dog-eared piece of paper which he smoothed out and handed to Luke.

"Here it is," he told him. "I had to keep this away from Adora. I was worried she might explode if she read it again."

Luke was silent for a time as he read the typed letter, his lips moving in concentration as he digested its contents. "I know he can be a little conceited, but this really doesn't sound like something Santa would write," he said.

"It's only natural that you want to stick up for him," Ben interrupted, "but it's all there in black and white. He's even signed it!"

"That *does* look familiar," Luke conceded, running his finger along the signature. Then he gasped in realisation and dropped the letter to the floor.

"I'VE GOT IT!" he shouted. "The signature! I know where I've seen it before!"

"Obviously," Ben replied. "Santa must write notes for you all the time."

Already running towards the stable door, Luke didn't reply. "Wait here!" he shouted as he hurtled through the door, leaving a *very* confused Ben behind.

***

After a few minutes, a panting and sweaty Luke returned. He pressed a piece of paper into Ben's hand and then doubled over with his hands on his knees, sucking in great big breaths.

"Read... that," he gasped, trying to get his breath back.

Ben began to read the letter and his heart sank as he realised that Luke had been telling the truth – Adora HAD written a letter to Santa! Ben felt guilty for doubting his friend, but also disappointed. He would never have expected Adora to be so *rude!*

"I'm sorry," he told Luke. "I guess they're both as bad as each other."

"That's not what I meant!" Luke told him. He took the letter from Ben and placed it on the ground, next to the letter from Santa. "Look at them together – what do you see?"

Ben knelt and studied the letters. The obvious similarity was how rude they both were, but then he noticed something else.

"It looks like they're both typed in the same font.

That's quite a coincidence."

"Is it?" asked Luke. "Or is it a clue? Look at the signatures."

Ben looked closely. Both signatures were signed in the same jet-black ink, but there were other features they had in common. The 'a' in both 'Santa' and 'Adora' was very distinctive, being a round circle followed by a prominent tail flick.

"The font, the pens, the signatures... It's like these letters have been written by the same person," Ben exclaimed, his eyes widening. "But who? And why? Who would want to cause this much trouble?"

Luke picked up the letters from Ben and leaned back against the reindeer stall. Placing his elbows on the fencing, he looked up at the sky, lost in thought. "I don't know, but if we find out then we can stop this whole crazy contest. Then we – **HEY! GET OFF!**"

Rudolph and Dancer had appeared at Luke's side and were acting very strangely. Normally they only behaved for Santa, but they sniffed Luke affectionately as they tried to lick him with their slobbery tongues.

"What's put you in a good mood?" wondered Luke as he hesitantly reached out to stroke Rudolph's head. Rudolph barely noticed – both he and Dancer were fixated on the letters that Luke held in his other hand. Their huge tongues crept forward like hungry snakes as they tried to lick them.

Luke pulled back and turned to Ben in confusion. "That's weird, they were just fed a couple of hours ago. What's so interesting about these letters?"

"It's *very* weird. I thought they were only interested in carrots."

The friends looked at the letters closely and noticed something that they had both missed before – faint orange smudges dotted around the paper.

"Carrot stains!" shouted Luke. "It must be! The reindeer can smell carrots from anywhere."

"Let's think this through," Ben told him. "Someone writes to both Santa and the Tooth Fairy. Someone who knows what happened at the Christmas party. And this mysterious someone eats carrots."

"THE EASTER BUNNY!" they shouted in unison,

hardly able to believe it.

"But he's their friend," Luke mused. "Why would he do something like that?"

"There's only one way to find out," Ben told him. "I think it's time we paid him a visit!"

***

"I still think we should have told someone we were coming," complained Luke.

"We've been through this," sighed Ben. "Neither Santa nor the Tooth Fairy would believe it was the Easter Bunny. And the quicker we sort this, the quicker things can go back to normal!"

The two of them nodded an acknowledgement at the rabbit who let them into the warren, then began to make their way down the tunnel. Practically every inch of the wall was covered by a lovingly painted mural. It depicted the Easter Bunny in various locations around the world, handing out beautifully painted eggs to adoring children.

"At least tell me we have a plan," said Luke. "We

can't just wander up to the Easter Bunny and ask, 'Are you evil?'"

"The first thing we need to do is find Martin," Ben told him. "If anyone knows what's going on with the Easter Bunny, it will be him."

The two walked in silence for a time, the tunnel gradually growing wider as it snaked towards the centre of the warren. Their stomachs rumbled as the delicious aroma of chocolate grew gradually stronger, telling them that they were close to their destination.

When they reached the mouth of the tunnel, Ben stopped and turned towards Luke.

"Now remember, we've got to keep a low profile. We don't want the Easter Bunny to know we're here until we have a better idea what's going on."

"Ben, you be- "

"Look, just keep calm. We're a great team – we can do this!"

"No, look be- "

"Stop worrying! We'll be fine!"

Luke didn't look convinced by Ben's assurances. He

looked as nervous as a Roman gladiator fighting hungry lions while dressed as a giant steak. A *very* tasty looking steak.

"What is it?" sighed Ben.

Luke wordlessly pointed over Ben's shoulder. Ben turned around to find the Easter Bunny standing in front of him, blocking the tunnel ahead.

"Hello boys," he smiled, showing his giant front teeth. "Are you looking for me?"

"We definitely should have told someone we were coming!" moaned Luke.

21

THE MOMENT OF TOOTH

"Where is that boy?" muttered Santa as he hurried through the empty corridors of the Tooth Fairy's castle. It was almost time to start that night's deliveries and he felt woefully unprepared. The fairy imps were no help at all, and Ben was nowhere to be found.

Was Ben upset with him? Was he with the fairy imps, watching him from afar and laughing at his predicament? Santa flushed with embarrassment as he recalled their distraught faces. He had to find a way to make it up to them!

But how? Without Ben he had no idea where to go,

or even where to start. What was he supposed to do – visit every house just in case a child had lost a tooth?

His mind made up, Santa turned on his heels and headed back towards his bedroom. It was hopeless to even try – children would just have to do without Tooth Fairy visits for one evening.

"I'm going to bed!" he shouted, in case any fairy imps were watching. "I don't have the foggiest what to do and none of you are any help whatsoever. So, *goodnight!*"

Although no fairy imps were visible, Santa could hear their agitated high-pitched whispers as he stomped across the room. Then a paper plane cut through the air, looping and turning before spiralling down and lodging itself inside his tiara.

Santa removed it and unfurled the paper to find that it was a list of that evening's deliveries.

"Well thank you *very much*," he told them. "Nice of you to finally be of some help. But what am I supposed to give them? A friendly pat on the head?"

The Tooth Fairy's bag was lobbed across the room, full to bursting with £1 coins. It caught Santa right in the middle of his ample stomach, knocking him down onto his oversized bottom.

Santa hauled himself up, the sound of the fairy imps' high-pitched giggles ringing in his ears. Clambering to his feet, he adjusted his dress and tiara as he tried to regain his dignity.

"Thank you," he sniffed. "Now if you'll excuse me, I have to be going. *Some of us* have to work!"

***

Santa was cold, tired and in a foul mood when he reached the first stop of the night. He'd had plenty of time to think on the long journey and had come to a decision. As soon as he finished his deliveries he was heading straight back to the North Pole, getting as far away from teeth as possible.

"I don't know what I'm even doing here," he grumbled as he checked the list. "They're only teeth for goodness sake!"

He crammed the list into his bag, still muttering to himself. "All this fuss for one measly pound! I bet most children hardly even notice it's there!"

Santa tapped his nose and within the blink of an eye vanished from the rooftop and appeared within a small bedroom. The pale moonlight peeking past the edge of the curtain picked out a young girl with curly red hair. She was sprawled out on the bed, her covers dishevelled and askew.

"Right then, let's get you sorted out," Santa whispered. He lifted the pillow and reached in for the tooth, but before he could grasp it the girl began to moan softly. Her cries grew louder, and her small body began to thrash from side to side.

Santa heard noises from the corridor and saw a sliver of light appear under the bedroom door. As the sound of approaching footsteps grew closer, he touched his nose and teleported himself outside. Activating his wings, he hovered outside the window, peering through the curtains and watching for a sign that it was safe to return.

Mrs Jensen knelt beside Sophie's bed and stroked her head, whispering heartfelt reassurances. Gradually, Sophie's cries quietened, and her weary eyes flickered open.

"I had a bad dream, Mummy," she sobbed, sitting up and throwing her arms around her Mum's neck.

Mrs Jensen held her tightly, rubbing her back and stroking her hair. "It's okay, Mummy's here now."

"My mouth hurts!" Sophie sobbed. "I can feel it with my tongue – there's a big hole and a really funny taste."

Mrs Jensen moved to sit on the bed, putting her arm around Sophie and pulling her close. "I know, but you're being super brave. If it upsets you having it here I can always take the tooth away."

Sophie pulled away from her Mum, looking horrified at the mere suggestion. "You can't do that, Mummy! I need to leave it for the Tooth Fairy."

"But if it's upsetting you?"

Sophie wiped her nose with the back of her hand. She lifted her pillow and checked underneath, reassuring herself that the tooth was still there.

"The Tooth Fairy needs my tooth – she collects them. If I can't have it anymore then I'm glad that it's going to someone who will take care of it."

Mrs Jensen smiled as she pulled her daughter close. "I'm proud of you, sweetheart. I hope the Tooth Fairy knows how lucky she is."

Later, when the house was in darkness and all was still once more, Santa appeared within the bedroom. He lifted the tooth from beneath Sophie's pillow and replaced it with a shiny £1 coin.

He smiled kindly at Sophie's sleeping form and then carefully examined the tiny tooth, a thoughtful expression on his face as he held it up to the light.

22

WELCOME HOME

Adora looped the ribbon through and pulled the bow tight, before standing back to admire her handiwork. What she saw in front of her made her want to cry.

The wrapping paper was not only askew but had been cut *far* too short. The ragged pieces were held together with huge chunks of Sellotape, with large portions of the present visible underneath. Whereas the elves' presents had beautifully folded smooth edges, Adora's were crumpled and misshapen. Even the ribbon was drooped over and lifeless, like a plant desperately seeking water.

The present looked like she had wrapped it blindfolded.

Using only her feet.

While having a sneezing fit.

Adora glanced at the clock on the workshop wall and groaned. It was almost midnight and she hadn't even started her deliveries. The elves were still on strike. She could hear them on the other side of the workshop door, marching back and forth and chanting *very* rude things about her.

She had been in the workshop for hours, attempting to do the work of the striking elves. It had *not* been easy. As terrible as it was, this sad looking present was her best effort yet.

Things might have been easier if Luke had been there to assist, but Adora had no idea where he'd got to. She'd tried asking the elves, but they had just joined hands and started to sing *Santa Claus is coming to town* at the top of their voices.

It was all too much for one person to do! Adora suddenly missed her home very much, longing to be back in familiar surroundings with her beloved fairy imps.

With a resigned sigh, she picked up the pieces of a toy car and began to assemble it. The task was going reasonably well until a small wheel pinged off and landed on the floor, rolling under a worktop. Cursing under her breath, Adora slid on to her belly and pressed herself against the floor, stretching to locate the wheel. She pulled up her red furry hood as extra protection in case she bumped her head.

Adora heard the workshop door burst open and then a familiar voice began talking ten to the dozen, barely pausing for breath.

"Christopher Claus! I know you're in here, there's no use hiding from me. You were meant to pick me up at the airport! Have you *any idea* how difficult it is to get a taxi to come all the way to the North Pole? I had to ride on a polar bear for the last stretch!"

Adora heard footsteps move closer and she stretched out one last time, her fingers brushing the edge of the wheel.

"Christopher, you're skin and bones! I knew I shouldn't have left you alone! You promised me you'd look after yourself, but I should have known you wouldn't take a break."

Adora felt her legs being gripped, and she was pulled backwards by strong hands.

"You've practically wasted away! You are not leaving this workshop until you've put on some weight. Stay here and I'll fix you up a nice meal."

Adora rolled over and stood up, drawing back her hood. "Hello Mrs Claus," she said. "How was your holiday?"

Mrs Claus was momentarily lost for words but quickly recovered, folding her arms and giving Adora a penetrating glare.

"You're going to tell me where my husband is and why you're wearing his clothes, and you better hope that I like the answer!"

***

"Children!" exclaimed Mrs Claus. "You're like a couple of children!"

Adora had filled Mrs Claus in on her feud with Santa

and the resulting job swap, and it was fair to say that Mrs Claus hadn't been impressed. She had rolled her eyes and tutted at various points, and her head was in her hands when Adora recounted the disastrous visit to the same house.

"Typical man," tutted Mrs Claus. "I leave him alone for five minutes and he manages to cause chaos."

She unbuttoned her thick red coat and laid it on a chair, removing her woollen hat to reveal a bun of grey hair. "So, how are you going to fix this mess?" she asked Adora.

"Me?" replied Adora. "Santa... I mean, your husband, started it."

Mrs Claus sighed and rolled her eyes. "My dear, that's what men do – they get a silly idea into their head and follow it through regardless of the consequences. It's a pride thing, you know."

"I suppose I should take some of the blame," admitted Adora. "I just got so angry with his boasting. We all know how much children love him!"

Mrs Claus gave a sad smile and moved to sit down

on a bench, beckoning Adora to come and sit next to her.

"My Christopher can be a bit of an exhibitionist at times, I'll give you that. But when he talks about children loving him it's not just because he likes the attention; it's because he's happy that he's given them something to look forward to."

Adora sat down beside Mrs Claus, drawn in by her story. "I don't understand. What do you mean?"

"I mean that all he's ever wanted to do is make children happy. Why do you think he works so hard? Why do you think he goes to all the effort of making such wonderful presents? Christopher knows that life can be hard at times, even if you are a child. That's why he tries to give them that one special day."

"I always thought that Santa had it so easy," admitted Adora. "These last few days have been a bit of an eye opener."

Mrs Claus took Adora's hand and gave it a friendly squeeze. "It's wonderful work – it's what gets him out of bed in the morning. But there have been sacrifices along the way. Did you know that we haven't always lived at the North Pole?"

"Really?" exclaimed Adora. "I didn't know that!"

"It's true. When we were first married we had a little workshop in Gmunden; then one year we visited the North Pole. That's when we discovered the elves and realised what a special gift they had for making things. Christopher realised that with their help he could make so many more children happy."

"Couldn't you have taken them back to live with you?" asked Adora. "It's freezing here!"

"No, that was never an option," Mrs Claus chuckled. "The elves would never have left their home, and I knew how much it meant to Christopher. I quickly grew to love it here as well – we finally had a family of our own."

"You really miss him, don't you?"

"I do," admitted Mrs Claus. "It's nice to get away for a bit of sun, but even nicer to come back home to loved ones. That's the only Christmas present I'll ever want."

She sighed and gazed into the distance. "I miss him so much, the silly old so and so. It's like I can almost hear his voice."

"HELLO!"

"As if he's right here with me."

"IS ANYONE THERE?"

"Right here in.... Wait, did you hear something?"

Adora and Mrs Claus turned as one, just in time to see Santa burst through the door. He was panting and red in the face, but he broke into a huge grin when he saw Mrs Claus. He flew over and wrapped her in a gigantic hug, lifting her off her feet.

"My darling – you're back! Oh, I've missed you so much my dear!"

Santa put Mrs Claus down and she stood there in shock, looking him up and down. Finally, she was able to regain her voice.

"Christopher, what on earth are you wearing?"

Santa looked down and blushed crimson, suddenly conscious of the fact that he was standing in front of his wife wearing a tiny pink dress.

"This old thing? It's part of the job.... That is, I.... You see..." Santa's words tailed off. "Do you like it?" he asked hopefully.

"I do," replied Mrs Claus, pinching his bottom and giving Adora a knowing wink. "I like a man in uniform."

***

Later, after Mrs Claus had left to unpack, Santa and Adora sat together and compared notes on their experiences. They alternated between listening with horror and erupting with laughter as they found what had transpired in their absence.

"I was wrong," admitted Adora. "Your job is a lot harder than I ever gave you credit for."

Santa nodded, grateful for the recognition. "And I must admit that I can see the importance of your job now. And I never thought I would say that about teeth!"

"Then we're agreed? We can stop this silly contest and go back to normal?"

"Believe me," replied Santa. "Nothing would make me happier!"

The old friends hugged; their earlier animosity

forgotten. "Come on," Santa said. "I'll give you a lift back. I can't wait to see my boys again."

When they reached the stables there was a cacophony of noise as the reindeer spotted their much-missed master. When he was finally able to extract himself from the onslaught of snuffles and licks, Santa set about getting the sleigh ready for flight.

"There's just one thing that I've found a little disappointing," he told Adora as he checked the harness. "Ben disappeared on me without even saying goodbye."

"Really?" asked a surprised Adora. "That's not like him. You know, Luke's vanished as well – do you think they could be together?"

Santa scratched his fluffy beard as he considered her words. "Maybe. I know they are very good friends."

"Garrooooh!!"

Santa chuckled as Rudolph shook his mighty head from side to side, snorting and emitting loud grunts. "Patience, Rudolph. We'll be in the air in no time!"

Adora kept her distance, happy to give Santa some

time with his beloved reindeer. She was somewhat surprised to see Rudolph acting so strangely – hadn't Luke told her that the reindeer always behaved for Santa?

She looked around the stable and her attention was drawn to something stuck on the wall in front of Rudolph – it looked like pieces of paper.

She pulled them down and frowned as she examined their contents. "Santa, come here," she called. "You have to see this."

Santa took the pages from her and his expression darkened as he read the top one. "This is that terrible letter you sent me! Why are you showing me this again? I thought we'd made up."

"Read the other one," Adora told him.

Santa spluttered incredulously as he began to read the second letter. "I didn't write this!" he shouted. "Who's to blame for this?"

"I didn't write the other letter either," Adora told him. "But the section on the bottom is *very* interesting."

Santa bent close to examine the letter. Below

'Adora's' signature there was a hastily scrawled note that read: "Letters from Easter Bunny. Gone to see him. Luke."

"The Easter Bunny?" Santa repeated in astonishment. "But why? That makes no sense at all!"

"I suggest we ask him," replied Adora. "How about it, Santa - shall we team up?"

Santa grinned and crouched down to place an arm around her shoulder. "Santa Claus is coming to town – and this time he's not alone!"

23

SECRETS, LIES AND EASTER EGGS

Santa and Adora crouched outside the entrance to the Easter Bunny's warren, watching his helpers scurry back and forth. Although Easter was still some weeks away it was clear that the preparations were already in full swing.

"Right, here's what we're going to do," whispered Santa. "You ring the doorbell and pretend to be a girl guide selling cookies. While they're talking to you, I'll sneak inside and search for Luke and Ben. When I find them, I'll grunt like a badger four times, then you- "

Santa tailed off as he realised that Adora was no longer beside him. Looking round frantically, he saw her strolling casually towards the front door.

"What are you doing?" he hissed. "That looks nothing like a girl guide uniform!"

"I don't like lying to people," Adora told him. "I always find that if you're nice to people then they'll be nice to you."

She marched up to the door and stepped in front of a young rabbit who was just exiting the warren. "Hello!" she said, flashing her brightest smile. "I wonder if you could help us. We're here to see the Easter Bunny – could you take us to him?"

The rabbit hopped nervously from foot to foot, looking around as if searching for reassurance. "I don't know... We're not really meant to let people in without an appointment."

Adora placed her hand on his shoulder and gave it a friendly squeeze. "Please – I'd appreciate it ever so much. We're old friends and it would be *so* nice to surprise him."

The rabbit thought for a moment before turning around and hopping back into the tunnel. "Come on!"

he shouted to Adora and Santa. "Follow me!"

***

Santa and Adora waved goodbye to the young rabbit and watched as he hopped up the tunnel and out of sight.

"Okay, what's the plan?" whispered Santa.

"We knock on the door, walk in and have a friendly chat," Adora told him.

"A friendly chat?" spluttered Santa. "That chocolate-rolling charlatan tricked us! And he kidnapped our helpers!"

"Remember that you're talking about one of our best friends," chided Adora. "There must be more to this than meets the eye."

It was obvious that Santa was less than convinced. His hands were clenched into fists and his ears were so red that Adora half-expected them to start emitting steam at any moment.

"Promise me that you won't do anything stupid," she urged him.

Santa didn't reply. Instead he scraped his black boots back and forth, like a bull about to charge. Then, with a deafening yell, he charged forward and burst through the door.

"Stop right there, you fiend!" he shouted. "This Christmas, I'm delivering PAIN!"

Adora rushed in behind him, only to be confronted with the strangest sight.

The Easter Bunny, Luke, Ben and Martin were all sitting together on comfortable leather sofas, sipping drinks. A depleted plate of biscuits lay on the table before them.

"What's going on?" asked a baffled Santa as he looked around him. "This doesn't look like a kidnapping."

The Easter Bunny put down his glass of carrot juice and hopped to his feet, smiling broadly as he faced his two friends.

"You did it! You actually did it!" He looked at Santa and his bottom lip began to tremble.

"Look at YOU! You look like... **HA HA**... You look

like... **HA HA HA**... You look... **HA HA HA HA HA HA!!!"**

The Easter Bunny dissolved into giggles and slumped to the floor, rolling around and clutching his aching sides.

"I did say that we should have swapped costumes first," Adora told an embarrassed Santa.

"Now look here," Santa chided, grabbing the Easter Bunny's arm and pulling him to his feet. "I want you to tell us what's going on here – right now!"

Wiping tears of mirth away, the Easter Bunny resumed his seat and gestured for Adora and Santa to sit down. They slid in between Luke and Ben, who gave them welcoming smiles.

"Let me start by saying that the two of you are my dearest friends, but you're both impossible! We've had to listen to you bicker with each other for years. Quite frankly we've grown a little tired of it!"

"Who has?" asked Adora.

"Everyone! Jack Frost, Sandman, Father Time, April Fool – and me, of course. You've spent hundreds of years debating who's best, when everyone else can see that you BOTH do an amazing job. That's why we came up with a plan."

"We?" roared Santa. "Which other friends stabbed us in the back?"

The Easter Bunny chuckled. "Oh, don't be so melodramatic! I came up with the idea of doing something, but it was April Fool who thought of the letters."

"These letters were really mean," complained Adora. "They said some terrible things."

Ben gave her hand a comforting squeeze and the

213

Easter Bunny squirmed in embarrassment.

"That was a mistake on my part. I thought the letters were so over the top that you'd realise they were jokes right away. I didn't think you'd start a gift-giving war!"

"I wouldn't call it a war," protested Santa. "Nothing too bad happened."

"I was almost squashed by a unicorn," Ben reminded him.

"And I came *very* close to ending up as a present," added Luke.

"Okay, *some* mistakes were made," Santa admitted. "But that doesn't explain the job swap. Why did you suggest that? Did you want us to fail?"

The Easter Bunny gave him an exasperated look. "I suggested it because after YOU KIDNAPPED ME, I realised that I had to calm things down. I thought that seeing how hard the other worked might stop your silly feud."

"And the costumes?" asked Adora. "Was it really necessary to swap?"

The Easter Bunny grinned cheekily as he looked at Santa's short pink dress. "Not really," he admitted. "But he did kidnap me, so I thought it was only fair that I got my own back."

"But you didn't stop there, did you?" Luke interrupted. "It was you who convinced the elves to strike!"

"And it was you who put the microphone in the kitchen!" added Ben.

Santa and Adora looked very confused with what they were hearing, but the Easter Bunny looked equally surprised. "My dear boys, I don't know what you're talking about."

"Yes, you do," protested Ben. "Admit it – you wanted both Santa and Adora to fail so that the Easter Bunny would be children's new favourite!"

The room erupted in noise, with everyone speaking at once.

"Bunny! Is this true?"

"I can't believe what I'm hearing!"

"How can you say that?"

215

"We're on to your game!"

"QUUUUUUIIIIIIIEEEEETTTTTT!!!!!!!!!"

Everyone stopped talking and turned to face Martin, who had been sitting quietly all this time. He looked nervous and upset, shrinking back into the sofa as if he wanted the thick leather to swallow him up.

"The Easter Bunny didn't do these things," he whispered in a small voice. "It was me."

24

THE NAUGHTY BUT NICE LIST

It was hard to tell who in the room was most taken aback by Martin's confession. Everyone sat in stunned silence, wondering if they had heard correctly. Martin had done this? Quiet little Martin?

The Easter Bunny was the first to react, hopping over to his friend and taking his hand. "Martin, what do you mean? Talk to us, my boy. You can tell me anything."

Santa opened his mouth to say something, but was quickly silenced by a dig in the ribs from Adora. "Let him talk!" she whispered.

"I'm sorry," sobbed Martin, tears beginning to well

up in his eyes. "I didn't mean to cause any trouble, not really."

"Well you did!" shouted Santa, unable to contain himself any longer. "Children almost missed out on their Tooth Fairy deliveries last night. How do you think that would have made them feel?"

Martin tightened his grip on the Easter Bunny's paw and looked sorrowfully at Santa and Adora.

"I didn't even think of that. I was so worried when the Easter Bunny went missing, and when I found out that you'd kidnapped him I wanted to teach you a lesson."

"Well I've got a lesson for you," snapped Santa. "You've just earned yourself a spot on the naughty list!"

It barely seemed possible, but this announcement made Martin look even more miserable. He let go of the Easter Bunny's hand and wearily stood up from the sofa, hunched over as if he had the weight of the world on his narrow shoulders. He mouthed 'Sorry' to Luke and Ben as he passed them, heading for the door.

"I'm sorry, Santa, but we can't let you do that,"

announced Luke as he stood up.

"That's right, there's no way Martin should go on the naughty list!" agreed Ben.

"Oh, so it's a mutiny is it?" said Santa. "You're all in this together, plotting to ruin me!"

"No, you silly old fool," Adora told him, not unkindly. "We're just trying to stop you from making a big mistake."

"People do silly things every day," Luke agreed, "but that doesn't mean they're bad."

"We all make mistakes sometimes," said Ben, "but what's important is that we learn from them."

The Easter Bunny had stayed silent throughout this discussion, but now politely cleared his throat. "And if we're looking for people to put on the naughty list, can I just remind you that you kidnapped me!"

Santa flushed with embarrassment and began to protest loudly. "That wasn't kidnapping! It was a silly mistake – I was tired and stressed and didn't know what I was doing!"

"That's our point," Luke told him. "Everyone does

some things that they're not proud of."

"I wrote naughty letters to my best friends," admitted the Easter Bunny.

"I suppose I may have been a *tiny* bit boastful," Santa grudgingly announced.

"And I destroyed the naughty list," admitted Adora.

"YOU DID WHAT?" screamed Santa.

The Easter Bunny jumped between his friends and took their hands. "The important thing is that we're all agreed that even the nicest of people make bad decisions sometimes. What do you say, Santa?"

Santa looked at the ceiling and puffed out his cheeks, before exhaling and counting to ten. He gestured to Martin, who was still standing by the door, watching the unfolding drama and unsure whether to stay or leave.

"I'm sorry, Martin," he told him. "I shouldn't have caused you worry like that – it was thoughtless of me. Will you forgive me?"

Martin gave a joyous shout and ran back into the room, throwing himself at Santa and giving him a massive bear hug that almost knocked him off his feet.

"It's quite alright my boy," Santa chuckled as he patted Martin's head. "You won't have anything to worry about anymore."

***

Luke, Ben and Martin stood and watched the festivities unfold around them. Santa's workshop was once again full of life and good cheer, with laughter and conversation having replaced shouting and angry words. The three friends tapped their glasses together in an unspoken toast, relieved that things appeared to be getting back to normal.

Adora was on the dance floor, surrounded by an adoring crowd of elves who had obviously decided to forgive her. The Easter Bunny was standing against the wall, chatting to April Fool and Jack Frost. Hoots of laughter drifted over as he recounted the shenanigans of the last few days.

Santa was in his regular position behind the drinks cabinet, while Mrs Claus crisscrossed the room, smiling and hugging old friends as she caught up on their news.

All seemed perfect and everything seemed to be right with the world once more. Friends had been reunited, job roles reverted to normal and – to the relief of everyone – Santa had finally changed back into his familiar red suit.

Then the music from the speakers cut out, replaced by a familiar voice.

"Thank you for coming tonight. It's wonderful to see so many good friends." Santa strolled through the crowded room, weaving past partygoers as he made his way to the stage. He climbed up the steps and looked out at the assembled guests.

"As it's such a special occasion, I've written a new song. This is about someone who works tremendously hard and is loved by children. I hope you like it."

Ben turned to Luke, his face a picture of horror. "Please tell me I'm dreaming! He's going to start the whole argument again!"

Luke couldn't find the words to answer. He saw

Adora fold her arms across her chest, obviously expecting the worst, and he willed Santa to do the right thing.

Santa cleared his throat and began to sing, his powerful voice echoing round the room.

"All around the world, children sleep in their beds
Hopes, dreams and wishes, filling up their heads.
When they come to wake up, what will they find?
A present that a certain special someone left behind."

Luke watched as Adora turned her back on the stage and walked towards the exit, shaking her head in frustration. "Why are you doing this, Santa?" he muttered.

"Every child knows that they can depend,
On that special someone who is their special friend.
There's no need to be afraid, there's no need to fear.
Because everything is better when the Tooth Fairy is here."

The room erupted with cheers and Adora turned back towards the stage, a look of pure astonishment on her face.

"Come on, Adora!" called Santa. "Get up here and join me!"

Adora grinned and flew towards the stage, swooping over the heads of her cheering friends. She landed on the stage and gave Santa a big hug, laughing as his bushy beard tickled her cheek.

"Well I'll be," announced Ben. "I guess this crazy week paid off after all."

"It's a Christmas miracle," laughed Luke, as he watched Santa and Adora begin a rousing rendition of *Santa Claus is coming to town*.

The boys put down their drinks and ran towards the dance floor to join their friends, while outside the brightest colours danced across the North Pole sky.

THE END

Dear Reader:

Thank you for reading *The Crazy Christmas Job Swap*. I hope you've had as much fun reading it as I did writing it! If you enjoyed the book, I'd be really grateful if you could post a short review on Amazon. Reviews are so useful in helping others learn about my books.

If you would like to see more examples of Julie Campbell's splendid illustrations, you can visit her website at http://www.juliecampbelldraws.com/

For information about my upcoming books and other publications, please visit my website at www.garysmithbooks.com, or follow me on Facebook at www.facebook.com/authorgarysmith/ I'd also love you to leave a comment letting me know your thoughts on the book and the answer to the most important question of all: are you team Santa or team Tooth Fairy?

Gary

Printed in Poland
by Amazon Fulfillment
Poland Sp. z o.o., Wrocław

50533693R00139